WISH AGAIN

THE WISHING TREE SERIES, BOOK 4

TAMMY L. GRACE

"I had planned on an early night but couldn't put this book down until I finished it around 3am. Like her other books, this one features fascinating characters with a plot that mimics real life in the best way. My recommendation: it's time to read every book Tammy L Grace has written."
— *Carolyn, review of Beach Haven*

"This book is a clean, simple romance with a background story very similar to the works of Debbie Macomber. If you like Macomber's books you will like this one. A holiday tale filled with dogs, holiday fun, and the joy of giving will warm your heart.
— *Avid Mystery Reader, review of A Season for Hope: A Christmas Novella*

"This book was just as enchanting as the others. Hardships with the love of a special group of friends. I

recommend the series as a must read. I loved every exciting moment. A new author for me. She's fabulous."
—*Maggie! review of Pieces of Home: A Hometown Harbor Novel (Book 4)*

"Tammy is an amazing author, she reminds me of Debbie Macomber… Delightful, heartwarming…just down to earth."
— *Plee, review of A Promise of Home: A Hometown Harbor Novel (Book 3)*

"This was an entertaining and relaxing novel. Tammy Grace has a simple yet compelling way of drawing the reader into the lives of her characters. It was a pleasure to read a story that didn't rely on theatrical tricks, unrealistic events or steamy sex scenes to fill up the pages. Her characters and plot were strong enough to hold the reader's interest."
—*MrsQ125, review of Finding Home: A Hometown Harbor Novel (Book 1)*

"This is a beautifully written story of loss, grief, forgiveness and healing. I believe anyone could relate to the situations and feelings represented here. This is a read that will stay with you long after you've completed the book."
—*Cassidy Hop, review of Finally Home: A Hometown Harbor Novel (Book 5)*

"Killer Music is a clever and well-crafted whodunit.

The vivid and colorful characters shine as the author gradually reveals their hidden secrets—an absorbing page-turning read."
— *Jason Deas, bestselling author of Pushed and Birdsongs*

"I could not put this book down! It was so well written & a suspenseful read! This is definitely a 5-star story! I'm hoping there will be a sequel!"
—*Colleen, review of Killer Music*

"This is the best book yet by this author. The plot was well crafted with an unanticipated ending. I like to try to leap ahead and see if I can accurately guess the outcome. I was able to predict some of the plot but not the actual details which made reading the last several chapters quite engrossing."

—*0001PW, review of Deadly Connection*

Wish Again
by
Tammy L. Grace

WISH AGAIN is a work of fiction. Names, characters, places and incidents either are products of the author's imagination or are used fictitiously. Any resemblance to actual events, locales, entities, or persons, living or dead, is entirely coincidental.

www.tammylgrace.com
Published in the United States by Lone Mountain Press, Nevada
Printed in the United States of America
ISBN 978-1-945591-29-7 (paperback)
ISBN 978-1-945591-28-0 (eBook)
FIRST EDITION
Cover by Elizabeth Mackey Graphic Design

For our wonderful readers in My Book Friends

ALSO BY TAMMY L. GRACE

WRITING AS CASEY WILSON

A Dog's Hope

A Dog's Chance

CHAPTER 1

*I*f not for the wet nose and hot breath on her arm, Paige would have stayed in bed. Gladys nudged her again, and despite the strong desire to pull the blanket over her head and spend another day hidden from the world, Paige threw off the covers and swung her legs over the side of her bed. Today was the day she had to reopen the bookstore. She had promised her brother.

She trudged downstairs, with the scent of lilies and roses growing heavier the closer she got to the kitchen. She opened the door to let Gladys into the backyard and gazed at the vases and baskets of flowers cluttering every surface. It had only been four days since her mother's funeral. The aroma heady and over-whelming, but the flowers were beautiful. A few pink rose petals littered the counter, shed like tears.

Margot had been a beloved member of the small community of Linden Falls, as was evidenced by the number of casseroles in the fridge and freezer, only outmatched by the flower arrangements. Friends and customers had packed the church for her service, all of them shocked at Margot's passing, especially so soon after that of Greta Harmon, another Linden Falls relic.

Thank goodness Jed had been there to accept the hugs and handshakes offered by everyone who had attended the reception after the service. He had been a rock and, alongside Tommy and Elise, his son and daughter, represented their family as their mother would have expected, while Paige had wilted. Her stomach had clenched and her knees had weakened as she stood in the receiving line next to her brother. In the midst of watching the never-ending line of men and women form, she had excused herself. She couldn't accept one more offer of condolence. Instead of staying at the church hall, she'd scurried out the back door and walked home. Embarrassed, she'd crawled into her bed with Gladys curled up beside her. She hadn't ventured from there for more than a few minutes since that day.

Despite Jed being only a year older than her, he had a bossy streak and all the characteristics of the stereotypical eldest child. He'd checked in on her immediately after the service and each day thereafter, forcing her to eat, but couldn't convince her to leave her room. She needed to wallow. Thinking she would be better, she had promised to open the store today. Now that Monday had arrived, she wasn't sure she could do it. The pain was too fresh, too harsh, too soon.

When she had moved back to Linden Falls in May,

she imagined spending years with her mother. She hadn't even gotten five months with her. Margot had been seventy-five, but she never seemed to age. She had been full of life, loved working in the bookstore and visiting with her customers, spending time with her friends that dubbed themselves the Winey Widows, and enjoying the town and people she thought of as family.

After Danny's death, Paige had come home at her mother's urging, so she wouldn't be in Albany alone. Her mother was right, Paige couldn't stay there. She had tried it for a few months, but it was miserable. She hadn't touched her sketch pad since the day of Danny's accident and had asked for extensions or cancelled all the books she had contracted to illustrate. As much as she knew she had to work, she couldn't bring herself to draw.

She also couldn't afford their house without Danny's income and didn't want to be reminded of all she had lost. Her whole life had been turned upside down, and when her mom offered her a place to stay, it had been the tiny push she needed.

Telling her handful of friends in Albany that she was moving back to her quaint hometown in Vermont, she had seen the doubt in their eyes. They couldn't understand and she hoped they never would. To understand it, they had to experience it, and she wouldn't wish that on anyone.

Losing Danny made her understand how strong her mother was when her dad had passed away. Margot didn't wither away. She'd poured herself into the store and kept going, surrounded by the town she vowed never to leave and the friends she loved. Tears trickled down Paige's cheeks as she thought about the trip she and her mom had planned for the spring. Her mom had told her about Driftwood Bay and the quaint cottages on the beach. She had made it sound idyllic, and Paige agreed that a change of scenery sounded wonderful. Her mom had visited the small town on the coast of Washington last fall with her group of friends, but she and Paige had an April trip planned, just for the two of them. That plan and so many others had vanished last Monday, when Paige found her mother in her bed, unresponsive.

Gladys wandered back to the door, her head and tail drooping as she continued to search for Margot. Paige had never been a dog person, not like her parents, who believed they were just like humans with fur.

Paige had grown up with dogs but had never paid them much attention.

Since she'd moved back home, she had a new appreciation and understanding of the role Gladys played in her mom's life.

This last week, since her mom's death, Gladys had been quiet and sullen, not her usual tail-wagging self. Like Paige, she too was grieving Margot's loss. She must have visited Margot's bedroom a hundred times a day and didn't understand when Paige didn't open the door to the bookstore, housed in a large section of the ground floor. On the rare trips Paige made downstairs, Gladys would station herself at the door and whine.

Paige caught herself before snapping at the sweet dog. She, of all people, should understand how distraught Gladys was. She had tried her best to tell her what had happened, that now it was just the two of them and she would need to adjust, but Gladys just stared at her with those big brown eyes.

In the end, Paige had slinked to the floor and rested against the door, sobbing, with Gladys's head in her lap.

She swiped the sleeve of her pajama top under her eyes, sighing at the fresh tears. How in the world could she manage opening the store today? She bent and petted the top of Gladys's soft head as they came into the kitchen. Paige filled the electric kettle with water and took out her favorite Earl Grey tea. Moments later the familiar tap on the back door made Gladys's tail wag. Jed and Bentley were here for their morning check-in.

Gladys could barely wait for him to open the door, and the moment it cracked open, the dark golden dog hurried through it, mauling Jed. His once blond hair was now gray, but the same twinkling blue eyes, exactly like their dad's, greeted her. "Hey, Paige. How ya doing?"

Gladys shimmied closer to Jed's dog, a sweet older golden named Bentley.

She shrugged. "I'm out of bed. That's about all I can say."

She nodded at the teakettle and raised her brows.

"I'd better pass. I need to get to the store. Just wanted to stop in and see if you needed anything. I took Tommy and Elise to the airport early this morning."

She sighed as she added the hot water to her mug. "I'm sorry I didn't even say goodbye." She shook her head. "I barely said hello. I've been in a fog for the last four days and don't remember most of it."

"It's okay. They understand." He glanced out the window. "It's supposed to rain this afternoon. I'll have one of the guys from the store come over with a load of wood and get it stacked under the porch."

His eyes drifted to the white mug with the spines of classic books decorating it. The one their mom had used each morning.

He quickly looked away and ushered Bentley out before scratching Gladys under her chin. "You take good care of Paige today." His voice caught and he waved goodbye before shutting the door.

His shoulders slumped as he walked away, his head bent toward the ground.

Jed was a caretaker, much like her dad had been. He was always making sure those he loved were comfortable and looked after and didn't hesitate to jump in and help. Not big on expressing his feelings with words, he did so through his caring gestures and work. He was always there for their mom, and she suspected he was heartbroken, maybe even more so than Paige, but he hid it better.

She ran her hand over her mom's mug before discarding her tea bag.

She padded into the large living room and out onto the porch that adjoined it. Tears stung her eyes as she wrapped her mom's warm shawl around her shoulders and nestled into the swing. The flowery scent of her mom's perfume lingered on the shawl and tickled her nose. She and her mom had spent almost every evening sitting on the swing, sipping wine as they watched their little world in Linden Falls go by.

Now Gladys curled up at her feet and Paige cradled the warm mug in her hands. She glanced across the square and saw the Wishing Tree, in all its autumn splendor. The canopy of brilliant orange and golds was stunning. Fall had been her mom's favorite season, and her upstairs corner bedroom gave her an unfettered view of the tree.

When Paige had lived in Albany, she often talked with her mom on the phone in the evenings, just before Margot turned in for the night. Her mother had remarked about the Wishing Tree and how much it comforted her. She'd loved that it was the first thing she saw each morning and the last thing she glimpsed before bed.

Years ago, at the urging of the neighbors and merchants surrounding the town square, the powers that be had agreed to install twinkly lights in the tree.

Margot always thought of the tree as her own giant nightlight.

Paige could see the multitude of wishes fluttering in

the breeze, hanging from ribbons attached to its branches. With rain expected, Neva would no doubt be out this morning, collecting all of them to save them from the impending showers.

Neva, with her long silver hair, had owned the Wishing Tree Inn as long as Paige could remember and was known as the Curator of Wishes. She took her job seriously, gathering the wishes and protecting them from inclement weather and keeping binders of them stored at the inn. Paige thought of her collections, decades old, as a sort of Museum of Wishes. Paige always judged Neva to be a bit unusual but kind. However, she was a good friend and neighbor to her mother and had been a loyal customer at the bookstore. They had common ground, too. Both of them were businesswomen, and they loved the Wishing Tree. While her mother had a peculiar attachment to the tree, even referring to it as *her*, as if it were a person, Neva took it to another level, making it the focal point of her life.

Paige had believed in all of her mom's stories about the huge tree granting wishes and went along with her mom crediting the tree for her marriage and had even tied her own wishes on its branches, hoping for a certain Christmas gift or good grade on a test or a prize in one of the many drawing contests she had entered. The tree had never failed to deliver, and like her mom, Paige trusted in its powers. That is, until that night so many years ago, when she lost all belief in the legends and magic.

The night her daddy had died.

The swing creaked as Paige let it sway her back and forth, her feet barely sweeping the porch floor. As she swung, the memories of that dark day surrounded her.

She and her mom had sat right here in this very swing after getting the news. Paige couldn't believe the Wishing Tree had let her down. She had sobbed in her mother's arms asking her how it could be. How could she ever trust the tree again?

A breeze made her shiver and ruffled her hair.

Paige could swear that, whispering on the wind, she heard her mom's voice, speaking the same words she had told her that tragic night.

"Wish again, sweetheart. Wish again."

CHAPTER 2

*A*fter a long, hot shower, Paige felt perkier. She summoned the energy to toss her stale bedding into the washing machine, then made another cup of tea and opened the door off the kitchen that led to the large bookstore her dad had built for her mom.

The mingled scents of fresh ink, paper, and the lingering fragrance of the sachets her mom carried brought her comfort. It felt like a hug from her mom, encouraging her that she could handle the hard day that lay before her.

She and Gladys made their way to the bright red front door, and she peeled off the sign someone had placed on the glass letting customers know they were closed. The deep fall colors of the mums she and her mom had planted in the wine barrels out front gave a stunning and cheerful welcome that Paige just wasn't feeling this first morning of work without her mom.

She took a deep breath and relaxed her shoulders in

preparation for what she knew would be a busy day of leaf-peeping tourists.

She went to the counter, a U-shape that carved out a niche along the wall with the door connecting to the kitchen, providing easy access to snacks, tea, or the powder room.

Gladys sniffed at her mom's chair, where another soft wrap, this one a deep merlot, was draped across the back of it.

Everywhere she looked she saw her mother.

Paige focused her attention on a small stack of boxes. They contained books they hadn't yet gotten to that needed to be checked and added to the inventory, then shelved. She vowed to keep busy instead of letting the memories overtake her.

She took the glass and stainless cordless electric kettle that she had splurged on from the counter along the back wall and filled it in the kitchen. With both of them working in the store, drinking tea, she'd thought the second kettle was a necessity.

Her hands shook as she positioned it on the pad and flipped the switch.

Muscle memory was a gift today and she used it while, mechanically, she turned on the computer, adjusted the volume on the background instrumental music her mother favored, bumped up the thermostat, and filled Gladys's water bowl. All tasks she and her mom completed each day without thinking.

And she didn't want to think.

She took a handled duster and ran it along the

bookshelves, stopping at the shelf reserved for all the children's books she had illustrated that her mother had proudly displayed with a little sign letting everyone know they were illustrated *by her daughter*.

She gave the knickknacks a quick swipe and tackled the framed prints decorating the walls alongside several of her own drawings of the Wishing Tree.

At her mother's request, she had drawn it during each season, and the large, framed colored pencil drawings were displayed across the front wall.

She straightened the desk and glanced at the family photos her mom kept nearby. There were a couple of old ones when she and Jed had been little and her parents so young. Her eyes locked on to the double folding frame her mom had treasured. It held their black-and-white wedding photo and another of them in front of the bookstore after the remodel, both smiling, their arms around each other.

Tom and Margot Duncan.

There weren't many couples like them and now they were both gone.

Paige dusted another frame, this one of her with Danny, holding hands and smiling. Another one showed Jed with his kids from a few years ago when they had spent all their summers with him in Linden Falls.

Margot had loved her grandchildren and had other framed memories scattered around her workspace.

Jed had chosen names that delighted their parents.

Tommy for Tom and Elise for Margot Elise.

Paige had hoped to add at least one more grand-child to the mix but, after three miscarriages, had been told there was no more hope. She and Danny had been devastated but had become even closer, pouring them-selves into each other. Now, without him, she was lost. She had just started feeling stronger, and now, her mom was gone.

She wasn't sure she could survive this.

Gladys rested her snout atop her thigh, offering her a bit of comfort. Paige closed her eyes and let the comforting scents from the store, the place her mom spent most of her waking hours, surround her. If she didn't open her eyes, she could pretend Mom was still there, checking on orders to make sure she had enough supplies and scouring the distributors for the latest books.

Keep it together, Paige.

She decided to let herself believe her mom was just on another trip and she was minding the store, like she'd done last year. She'd be fine until customers mentioned Margot and told her how sorry they were.

Paige would have to prepare herself for those well-meaning sentiments, because they would be coming fast as soon as the town woke up.

It wasn't long before two of the big tour buses eased down Main Street, dropping off their passengers before driving down the road to park in the field of an entrepreneurial farmer. She was glad he'd discovered a way to make extra money during the tourist season.

Many of the passengers stood in the square, getting

their bearings, admiring the Wishing Tree. Some of the groups headed off to the small gift shops dotting the street, others to the coffee shop or café, but there were always more than a handful who made a beeline for the red door of Town Square Books.

The next few hours passed in a blur, as Paige helped customers find books, suggested a few for those looking for something to read, and rang up sale after sale.

With all the commotion, Gladys made her way to the door and slipped out when one of the customers left with a heavy shopping bag on her arm. Paige saw her but didn't worry. Gladys liked to roam the square most days, stopping in to get a quick pet or a treat from the shopkeepers she knew while on her way down the street to Duncan's Hardware, where she'd spend part of the day with Jed and his dog, Bentley.

Sometimes Bentley returned with her, but more often Gladys would come back alone in the middle of the afternoon, in time for a long nap before the store closed. Margot had chosen the name Gladys as an homage to the character in *Bewitched*, because she had been such an inquisitive puppy. Turned out she didn't outgrow it and was still a nosy dog, always poking her head into the doorways of the shops and houses surrounding the square. She knew everyone and everyone knew her. If she became a nuisance, they'd send her on her way, but most everyone loved the sweet girl.

Paige was happy to see Gladys back to her old

habits, instead of sticking close to her and wallowing, like she'd done over the last week.

Paige couldn't imagine what the poor dog thought without her person there or how she'd suffered in confusion as, together, they'd watched the paramedics carry Margot downstairs and out to a waiting ambulance. Gladys had whined in tune to Paige's crying.

There was nothing they could do, and Paige had known that even as she dialed 911 and asked for the ambulance.

When the dust had settled, Paige considered Gladys. The last thing she needed was a dog to take care of while she managed the bookstore alone, but over the last week, that thought had changed.

Gladys wasn't just a dog who shed golden fur all over the dark wooden floors and needed walking and picking up after, who would complain if her dinner was late. She was a true comfort and a loyal companion. Paige wasn't sure if the training that Gladys had completed to get certified as a therapy dog was the reason, but she suspected it helped.

During the lunch hour, Paige had a short reprieve from customers, who packed into the small cafes and restaurants around the square. After nibbling on some leftovers and an excellent piece of pound cake, she started the fire her brother had thoughtfully laid in the fireplace.

The sky had darkened and the pleasant smell her mother loved to remind her was known as petrichor filled the air. Despite having never gone to college, her mother had been a master of words and vocabulary, which came from her love of books.

Paige poked the button on the answering machine and poised her pen over a notepad as she listened to dozens of messages. Several were from people expressing their sorrow and offering condolences. Others were about orders from customers who didn't know Margot was no longer there.

A message from Faith at Aspen Grove, the care center and assisted living facility where Margot and Gladys volunteered, asking if Paige would be able to make her scheduled time on Thursday this week, brought tears to Paige's eyes.

She hadn't gone with her mom when she made her Thursday and sometimes weekend trips to the facility. She hated the smell of those places like she hated the smell of hospitals. She couldn't bring herself to visit. The short time Danny had spent in the care center in Albany had been enough to last her a lifetime. He was one of the youngest patients there, and she had watched him slowly fade after the accident and eventually give up the fight. After that, she wished with all she had that she would never have to make the decision to put another person she loved in one of them.

Ironically, now she didn't.

Dread washed over her, and her stomach knotted around the cake she'd enjoyed. She wasn't trained with Gladys and couldn't possibly pick up her mother's obligations at Aspen Grove, not with everything else to do. How had her mother done it all?

She dialed the number Faith had left, unsure of how to tell her she couldn't continue. Faith's cheerful greeting and sincere expression of sympathy made it harder. "We just loved Margot and can't believe she's gone. I hated to bother you, but the residents are just heartbroken and have been asking about Gladys. They're worried about her, too."

"Oh, yes, it's been such a shock. I'm just not sure I can continue. I'm not trained in handling Gladys and would hate to do something wrong."

"Oh, no need to worry on that front," Faith said. "Gladys knows what to do. She'll show you. She's always so happy visiting all the residents, and she'll make sure they all get a chance to pet her. They adore her. Of course, we understand if Thursday is too soon, but we can make any day work, whatever is convenient for you. Everyone really looks forward to her visits."

"Is there anyone else who can cover with another therapy dog?"

"I'm afraid not. Margot is...*was* our only volunteer. It would mean so much if you could find it in your heart to continue, or at least give it a try. Your mom was so very special and so loved."

Tears leaked from Paige's eyes as she swallowed the lump in her throat. She couldn't say no. She couldn't disappoint her mom. Her mother had even adjusted the hours at the bookstore with a late opening at noon on Thursdays to give her time for her visits at Aspen Grove.

Paige sighed. "I'll be there, but I might need some help."

Faith sounded relieved. "I'll be by your side the whole time. Just come to the main entrance at nine o'clock and I'll be there. I can't wait to meet you."

Paige wrote down the address, thanked Faith, and disconnected. She looked at her mom's planner on the desk with Thursday blocked out each week. Her mother's perfect handwriting had lettered in *Aspen Grove* on each square of the calendar. She'd looked forward to her trips, often squeezing in a second visit on Sundays. Her mother always came home happy and had asked Paige on more than one occasion to come with her, citing what a wonderful place it was and how happy Gladys made the residents, but Paige had never gone.

Deep in her heart, Paige knew her mother would want her to continue her work.

She wandered over to the window facing the square and saw Neva collecting the last of the wishes, just as the first drops of rain dotted the streets. The breeze had picked up, and Neva was struggling to hang on to all of them but hurried back inside the bed-and-breakfast, leaving the Wishing Tree branches bare of ribbons and paper.

Inside the store, it was busier than ever with people crammed into every corner, not wanting to be outside in the rain. Several of them camped out in the comfortable chairs her mother had positioned around the space, reading the books they had just purchased.

Soon, the buses reappeared and the store emptied.

Gladys had slipped back inside when the customers were boarding the bus and was lounging in front of the fire, drying her fur. Not that the rain bothered her much. The natural oils in her coat repelled it, and after a few minutes, you would never guess she had been out in the weather. The snow was her absolute favorite, according to Margot. She had made Paige laugh telling her about Gladys using her snout to make huge tunnels in the backyard last winter and even texted her some photos. Her mother couldn't wait to show Paige how excited Gladys got for the first snowfall.

Now, it would just be the two of them.

Paige bent down to pet her and Gladys rolled onto her back, giving her easy access to scratch her belly. She ran her hands over it, admiring the long, almost-white feathers on it and on her tail. Paige reached to get a couple of stray leaves that were clinging to her. When she pulled them off, she noticed a ribbon tied to a piece of paper snared on their stems.

It appeared that Neva had missed one of the wishes.

She unfolded the paper, glad it was protected by Gladys's furry tail and was dry and readable.

Please comfort my mom, Hazel, who I've had to leave at Aspen Grove. She won't leave Linden Falls and can no longer care for herself but needs a friend or two to watch over her. I hate leaving her, but she won't move to Boston, and it would ease my worry if I knew someone cared about her. –Robert

"Well, Robert, as luck would have it, Gladys and I will be at Aspen Grove this week. We'll have to look in

19

on Hazel while we're there." Paige shook her head as she looked at Gladys. "It's almost like Mom is making sure we go, isn't it?"

Gladys sat, listening to Paige.

Her pink tongue poked out of her mouth and her jaw lifted a bit, as if smiling. Her answer to Paige came in the form of several loud thumps of her tail against the wooden floor.

Paige couldn't help but smile, and when she bent down to pet her, Gladys rested her head on Paige's shoulder.

CHAPTER 3

*B*y Thursday morning, Paige had managed to put clean sheets on her bed and fold the ones she had laundered. She also had disposed of all the wilted flowers from her mom's service and stashed her favorite casseroles from well-wishers in the freezer after making sure Jed took his share home.

She reminded him to return all the dishes to their rightful owners, a task given to him since she wasn't sure she could handle more pity hugs and sad smiles.

She and Jed had taken to eating dinner together each night, but she wasn't sure how long that would continue. She hated to ask him but hoped he'd keep coming. It was nice to have someone to talk to at the end of the day.

Not to say that Gladys wasn't a good companion or an excellent listener, but Paige enjoyed hearing about her brother's work, and he made her feel safe.

She finished her tea and rinsed the mug before

putting on Gladys's harness her mom used when she took her to Aspen Grove. Gladys stood patiently while Paige struggled with the straps but finally got them snapped into the buckles.

Gladys pranced out to the garage and stood at the door of her mom's SUV. Paige wasn't ready to drive it yet, though.

That was going to take more time, so she guided Gladys to her own smaller SUV in the next stall.

Less than ten minutes later, she followed the signage for the Aspen Grove campus and pulled into the parking lot with Gladys's tail in full swing.

The dog was much more enthusiastic than she was.

However, she had to admit, the grounds were gorgeous, with lush green lawns adorned with beautiful fall flowers, along with the colorful leaves on the trees surrounding the acreage and walkways. It truly was a campus, with several white clapboard buildings in a farmhouse style, all with green shutters, that gave it a homey feeling.

Paige didn't need to follow the signs since Gladys led her right to the main entrance. When they walked through the door, a cheerful woman with short blond hair, dressed in colorful scrubs adorned with pink and red hearts, smiled at her.

Gladys tugged on the leash and hurried to the woman, who knelt down to pet her. "Aww, how are you, sweet girl?"

The woman, with deep blue eyes that forced anyone meeting them to smile, stood and extended her hand.

22

"You must be Paige. I'm Faith and I'm so happy you're here." She glanced down at the dog. "Both of you."

Faith led them down the hallway and pointed out the administrative offices and her own office. "I'm never there, but that's where I pick up my phone messages." She slipped a card from her pocket. "I put my personal cell number on the back, so feel free to call me anytime."

They followed Faith farther, to the modern great room, where several residents were seated. Some were reading, others were knitting, and a few more were playing games or puzzles at the tables near the window.

A huge fireplace dominated the room and made it pleasant and toasty.

Gladys was eager to greet her favorites, and when they noticed her, smiles filled their faces.

The dog sure knew the drill, and she waited for Faith to tuck her leash into one of the zippered pockets on her harness.

"Gladys is a gem and will just go around and greet everyone. She doesn't need the leash in here."

Faith went on to explain that the residents there were ambulatory and lived in their own small apartments in the main building. Aspen Grove provided their meals and made sure they took their medications, took care of all their housekeeping needs, and provided lots of social activities.

Paige's brows rose in surprise when she learned there was a coffee bar, café, a salon with a barber, hairdresser, and nail technician, and even a gym on the premises.

"If their situation changes and they need medical care, either short-term or long-term, we can just transfer them to one of our other buildings, where we offer skilled nursing, rehabilitation, memory care, and even end-of-life care."

Faith smiled at a woman who was bending over her knitting to kiss the top of Gladys's head. "Sometimes they just need short-term care to recover from an illness or injury and then they move back here. We try to offer them a homelike setting and the security of knowing anything they need is right here on the campus. It gives them and their families peace of mind."

"It's quite lovely. I, uh, well, I expected something much more institutional and scarier." Paige shrugged. "Hospitals and care homes are not my thing."

Faith nodded. "I understand. When we go to the other buildings, the long-term care unit and the memory care unit are probably more like that institutional feeling you were expecting, but we pride ourselves on our care and environment. We'll have to keep Gladys on a leash in the other units."

Paige hung back, not wanting to intrude on the joy-filled reunion they were all having with Gladys, but more so because she wasn't sure she could handle hearing her mother's name. That was the problem with a small town; everyone knew her mom and the bookstore. They were all intricately connected and there was no escape, no anonymity.

It wasn't like in Albany when Danny had died. Only his coworkers and their small circle of friends were impacted. She had been able to go almost anywhere without anyone saying a word or offering a sorrowful smile.

As she watched Gladys delight in the attention with all the residents huddled around her, reaching to stroke her back or massage her soft ears, Paige smiled and had an inkling of why her mother took this volunteer work so seriously.

The joy Gladys was able to deliver, without saying a word, was nothing short of miraculous. It warmed Paige's heart to see their enthusiasm and hear their laughter when Gladys flopped down and rolled over for a belly rub.

The dog was a natural entertainer!

When Gladys had made the rounds and visited each and every person gathered in the common room, Paige followed Faith's lead and wandered closer to collect her. One of the women with snow-white hair and a huge blue and green broach and matching earrings smiled at her.

"Your dear mother was an angel. I can see you were lucky enough to inherit both her beauty and kind heart. Thank you for bringing our dear friend Gladys."

Tears stung Paige's eyes and she nodded, not certain she could speak without causing them to fall.

The group smiled at her as she took the leash from

Gladys's harness and led her back to the hallway, following Faith. She waited and held open a side door that connected to the long-term care center.

As they walked, Paige remembered the wish she had found in Gladys's tail.

"Faith, I just learned about a patient here named Hazel, who has a son named Robert. He lives in Boston. Do you happen to know her?"

Faith smiled and pointed at the building they were about to enter. "Yes, I do. She's actually in this building. She's new to us and is ill and needs skilled nursing care. She's a sweet one and hasn't met Gladys yet, but I'm sure she'd love to."

When she opened the main entry door, the smell of something like cinnamon or apples or maybe both drifted through the air. Unlike the antiseptic and musty odor that was always present at the place Danny had been, Paige was surprised at the pleasant and inviting aroma.

Faith led the way and explained that patient rooms were in two wings, with a common dining room and a smaller gathering place for television and socializing in the center.

She pointed out the alcove near the common areas where visitors could help themselves to juices, coffee, tea, and homemade apple cider, which explained the lovely scent.

Paige noticed several residents in wheelchairs navigating the hallways and only a handful watching television or reading. Faith pointed to one hallway. "Let's start down here and we'll keep hold of Gladys and pop into a few rooms where I know the patients are anxious to see her. Then we'll hit Hazel's room last."

Paige held her breath as they went into the first room. This was tougher than the other building, as most of these patients were frailer, dressed in hospital gowns, and confined to their beds.

Gladys wasn't deterred as she made her way to the side of their beds, taking care to place her nose next to their hands. With her gentle eyes, she looked upon them, transmitting her love. A twinkle in their tired eyes and their genuine smiles made Paige's throat go dry.

As they meandered down the hallway, Paige noticed that they left all of the patients a bit happier than when they had found them. They loved on Gladys and she relished the attention, smiling as they lavished her with snuggles and kind words. It was hard to leave them, knowing so many would be alone.

When they asked, Paige didn't hesitate to promise to return again next week.

Faith took them to the last room.

There was Hazel.

She was alone, sitting almost straight up in her bed, looking out the window, an open book across her lap and a fuzzy pink sweater over her gown.

Faith introduced Paige.

"Hello, Hazel. Would you like a short visit with me and my dog, Gladys?" Paige asked.

The confusion in her rheumy blue eyes was

replaced with happiness. "I would love it," she said, gesturing to the chair next to her bed.

They stepped forward and Gladys squeezed next to the side of the bed, within easy petting distance. The faint aroma of lavender surrounded Hazel, and Paige noticed the tube of hand cream on her bedside table, along with a vase filled with purple and yellow flowers.

Faith excused herself and asked Paige to find her before she left for the day.

Hazel reached out and ran her fingers over the top of Gladys's head, smiling when she moved to her ears. "They're like velvet, aren't they? What a sweet girl. I haven't had a dog in years, but oh, how I love them."

Paige nodded. "I grew up with dogs but haven't had one on my own. Gladys belonged to my mother, but now we're becoming fast friends." She gestured to the vase. "Those flowers are gorgeous."

Hazel smiled and said her son had sent them. She went on to explain she lived in a small town a few miles away and had one son, Robert, who lived in Boston. "He wanted me to move to a facility in the city, but I love it out here in the gorgeous countryside. I want to spend my last days where I've always been the happiest, and I heard great things about this place."

"Today's my first day volunteering and first time here, but I'm impressed. Everyone on the staff seems great," Paige said.

Hazel nodded, her short, wispy gray hair making her look like an older version of a pixie. Gladys rested her head on the blanket next to Hazel's skinny arm, hooked up to an intravenous unit dripping clear liquid into the line. "Robert didn't want to leave me here. I know I upset him, but he doesn't understand. I know it will be hard for him to visit often, but I'm at peace here and love the view and being close to home."

Paige relaxed her grip on the leash. "I understand. I grew up in Linden Falls but just moved home this summer to live with my mom."

She glanced at her watch. "In fact, I need to get going and open the bookstore."

"You must mean Town Square Books?" Hazel's eyes brightened. "Are you Margot's daughter?"

She smiled and nodded. "Yes, you know the store?"

"Oh, my, yes. I've spent many an afternoon in there reading and visiting." Her eyes lost focus and got a faraway look in them. "I made the trip to Linden Falls for shopping and whatnot a few times a month and always tried to stop in the store and browse." She laughed. "More like buy. Margot and I would visit over a cup of tea or sometimes a maple creemee from Doc's." She winked and Paige glimpsed a hint of what she must have been like in her younger years. "Margot had a fun knit and crochet group that met there at times, as I recall. How is your mom? You mentioned Gladys is her dog?"

Paige swallowed hard, followed by a deep breath. "My mother passed away unexpectedly last week. I moved here this summer after my husband died. Now…" Her voice cracked and she couldn't continue.

Hazel reached out a hand, the top of it covered with

age spots and lumpy blue veins that were amplified by her tissue-paper-like skin. She ran her fingers over the top of Paige's hand. "Oh, my dear, I'm so very sorry. I've been ill this entire year and haven't been to Linden Falls. I've been in and out of the hospital this last month and haven't kept up with the newspapers. Or I never would have asked."

Paige couldn't contain the tears that fell from her eyes. She tried to reassure Hazel with a smile but had to press her lips together to keep from sobbing.

Hazel grabbed her box of tissues from the wheeled tray across her bed and set them in Paige's lap. "You just cry all you want. When I lost my mother, I couldn't quit crying. There's nothing to be ashamed of, dear."

Paige plucked several tissues from the box and dabbed her face. Gladys moved closer to her and placed her head on Paige's thigh, doing her best to comfort her while keeping an eye on Hazel.

Hazel unwrapped a clean plastic cup from the stack on her tray and poured it half full of water from her pitcher, her arm shaking the whole time.

She handed it to Paige with a small nod. "I'm the baby in my family and the last one left. Nobody tells you how hard that will be when you're soaking up all the attention and being spoiled by everyone when you're growing up. I can't tell you that the hollow feeling in your heart will ever disappear, but time does lessen the sting. I was about your age when I lost my mom, but she was eighty-five. I still felt I didn't get enough time with her."

Paige took a few sips of water and settled in to listen to Hazel talk about her childhood and growing up on a farm with her brothers and sisters. She'd also lost her husband more than twenty years ago, so it had been just her and Robert for a long time.

Hazel chuckled and added, "I'm eighty-one now and doubt I'll make eighty-two, but inside, I've never felt old. Sometimes I'm quite shocked when I look in the mirror and see my wrinkled skin and almost white hair. I'm still the young girl who loved to run alongside the horses into town, swim in the creek, and bake cookies with my mother. Inside, I don't think I've aged a bit."

Time had evaporated as Hazel talked, and when Paige glanced at her watch, she gasped. "We need to get going so I can open the store. We'll be back next week to see you."

Hazel nodded and smiled, reaching out her hand for Paige's. "I appreciate you listening to me and letting me ramble on. It's lovely to have someone to talk to."

Paige squeezed her hand and took note of the book Hazel was reading, an older one by Debbie Macomber. "You take care, and we'll see you again soon."

She let Hazel pet Gladys one more time and waved goodbye, stepping into the hallway and searching for Faith.

One of the nurses caught Paige's eye and said, "Faith is back in the main building and said to let you know."

She thanked her and hurried out the side door. She

only had thirty minutes before the store opened and didn't want to be late.

Faith was signing a clipboard a nurse was holding for her, and when she turned around, Paige and Gladys were only a few steps down the hallway. "How did it go with Hazel?" she asked.

"Great. She's wonderful. I think she enjoyed the visit. I told her we'd be back next week. I've got to get moving so I can open but wanted to thank you."

Faith waved her hand. "No, thank you for being willing to come. I thought you might change your mind when you saw the impact Gladys has on the residents. They truly love her. You're welcome anytime. I'm off some weekends, but if I'm not here, just ask for my assistant, Penny. She covers when I'm gone and knows the ropes."

"Sounds great and I see why my mom loved coming here." She smiled at Faith, and before she knew it, Faith had her arms wrapped around her in a tight squeeze.

When she released her, Faith shrugged. "I'm a hugger, sorry. It's my way of letting you know how much you mean to me."

Tears stung her eyes again, and before she melted into a puddle, Paige waved goodbye and hurried Gladys to the car. That pink tongue of hers was hanging out and she was panting a bit, which always made her seem like she was smiling.

In the car, Paige rested her forehead against Gladys.

"Thank you for coming with me today," she whispered.

CHAPTER 4

O ver the next few days, the store was busy, which kept Paige's mind occupied. Her mom's friends must have all coordinated and scheduled to drop in and visit, because over Thursday, Friday, and Saturday, the Winey Widows all made an appearance, staying to chat over a cup of tea.

Jean was heading to Florida for the winter next week but promised to set up lunch when she returned in April and made Paige add all of their numbers to her cell phone.

Norma, who had been a school librarian and developed a strong bond to Margot over books, delivered some fresh-baked cookies with her visit. She was a wonderful knitter and offered to spearhead getting the knitting and crocheting group up and running for the fall and winter months. With the winter weather intense, it was a great way to pass the time, and the women loved gathering at the bookstore, with the warm fire and all the tea they could drink.

Cecilia and Agnes didn't cook much but stopped by the bookstore at the end of the day. They had just come from dropping off a meal at Henry and Greta's house. Agnes clucked as she unearthed a bottle of wine. "That poor man, he worked so hard to care for her. I worry about him."

Cecilia nodded. "I know Greta didn't cook much in the last year, and he probably got used to fending for himself, but at least we've let him know he's not forgotten." She sighed as she took the wine Agnes had poured. "Norma and Jean made most of it, but we went by the bakery and added some of those delicious rosemary sea salt rolls and a pie and dropped it all off."

Agnes handed Paige the tallest glass of wine she'd ever held before taking a gulp from her own glass and then dribbling in the last of the bottle and settling into a chair. "Of course, we didn't stay, but Henry seemed pleased with the meal. We'll have to make sure and drop over with something each week."

"I've got plenty of casseroles in the freezer and would be happy to gift him one. He was always a sweet man and I remember them coming into the bookstore years ago." Paige didn't mention to them that Neva was making sure that Henry had hot meals, too. She'd seen Janie's daughter, Breeze, headed over there on several occasions carrying dishes draped protectively with Neva's recognizable black-checkered dishtowels.

Telling them that would be gossip. At that decision

to keep the tidbit to herself, she could just see her mother's nod of approval.

As they sipped, the three of them shared stories about Margot. They all shed tears and laughed at memories of the woman they had all loved and held in high esteem. As they were getting ready to go, right before Jed arrived for dinner, Agnes raised the idea of continuing their Winey Widows meetings at the bookstore.

Cecilia poked Agnes with her elbow hard enough to make her squeal, but she quickly apologized.

Paige hadn't actually participated in their gatherings but had been within earshot of their conversations and knew how much the women and their "meetings" had meant to her mom. She told them both they were more than welcome to use the space and she'd expect them on Monday night, as usual.

Cecilia had stopped by again on Saturday, this time with lunch from Cobblestone, the small bakery and deli down the street. Over the most delicious paninis filled with maple turkey, ham, and cheddar, Cecilia apologized again for Agnes bringing up their meetings. She wanted to make sure it wouldn't be too upsetting to have them meet at the bookshop every Monday evening.

Paige's heart felt lighter and her mind in a better place by the time she flipped the sign over to CLOSED and locked the door. She had feared talking with them or mentioning her mom would only intensify her feelings of loss, but instead it put her more at peace and made her feel closer to her mom.

The visit to Aspen Grove on Thursday had sparked something inside Paige, something she liked to think was her mom's kindness spurring her on, making her realize how good it felt to do something for someone else. Someone like Hazel, who was truly alone.

Tears clouded her eyes as she went through the sales reports on the computer and filled out the deposit sheet. If Hazel had been her mother and, like Robert, she had to leave her alone, she would want more than anything for someone to spend time with her and take an interest in her. It would be depressing enough to be in a care facility, but to be alone, without family, would be downright frightening.

With Hazel on her mind all day, Paige gave a lot of thought to which books the woman might enjoy. She chose a few large-print editions with soft covers that were lighter and easy to hold, hoping they would brighten Hazel's day and provide an escape from sitting alone.

She took the stack of books she'd selected for Hazel and put them in a signature red bag with the black Town Square Books logo, added tissue, and tied it with a pretty gold ribbon.

With the gift bag ready, she closed up the store, and Gladys followed her into the main house. Knowing she'd have the next day off and would get to spend part of it with Hazel felt good. It would be so much better than sitting around the house, missing her mom.

"Eat up, Gladys," Paige encouraged the dog. "I want to make sure you are fat and sleepy while I'm gone."

Jed had decided they had eaten enough funeral casseroles for the week and insisted they meet up at the town favorite, Crooked Porch Café, for dinner.

Gladys finished her chow and Paige put her bowl in the sink, then began her walk across the square to meet her brother.

The sun-filled day gave way to a perfect fall evening, and the Wishing Tree was glowing with tiny white lights among her colorful leaves. Despite the grudge she held against the tree, she couldn't deny her beauty. It frustrated Paige that she still thought of the tree as a woman, never breaking from her mother's habit of assigning a female pronoun to the graceful tree.

Still, Paige stopped under the full branches, admiring the wishes Neva had retied after the rainstorm, fluttering on their ribbons. Paige hated to admit it, but *she* had given her a gift in that wish that had been tangled in Gladys's tail. Part of her had wanted to ignore it, but she would never think of punishing Hazel or Robert due to her personal grievance with the tree.

Maybe there was more to the tree than expecting it to deliver for her. Perhaps part of the allure was in the power of being the one to grant a wish.

Paige had never taken a wish off the tree before now and hadn't even considered it, relying on her belief, and that of her mother, in the power of the tree. She was old enough now to understand that people in town had actually been the ones to provide bicycles for kids who wished for them.

The tree wasn't a mythical fairy godmother who could wave her wand and make a bike appear. Paige still thought that her mother's belief in the idea of a bit of magic associated with the tree, no matter how beautiful and infamous it was, was farfetched.

With that thought, a bronze-colored leaf fell and landed on her shoulder.

She picked it up and twirled the stem in her hand, unable to turn her eyes away from the gorgeous lights and the wishes swaying in the gentle breeze.

Remembering that Jed would be waiting impatiently, she dropped the leaf and hurried across the square.

➤➤➤

SUNDAY DAWNED with sunshine and clear blue skies, and Paige treated Gladys to a long walk through town, then fixed her a generous breakfast, adding some scrambled eggs to the bowl of kibble.

"Spoiled much?" she asked the dog as she waited for her to finish.

Gladys ignored the question, but she ate with gusto, then took to her bed and napped while Paige took a shower and got ready for the day.

Once presentable, Paige checked the time, then plucked the book she was reading from the table before settling in to read.

She had used Robert's wish as a bookmark, and now she smiled at the ribbon nestled in between the pages.

The love he had for his mother was evident in his scrawled, heartfelt words.

Paige took a sip of tea and settled in for an hour of reading before heading to Aspen Grove.

From all the information Faith had provided, she knew they served Sunday lunch early at eleven and didn't want to interrupt the few hours the residents had to enjoy their meals.

Just after noon, she loaded Gladys into her SUV and drove down the street to Doc's Fountain, where she ran inside and ordered two maple creemees in to-go cups.

The prospect of surprising Hazel brought a ripple of excitement and a smile to her face. She exceeded the speed limit a bit, just to make sure the creemees didn't melt, and pulled into the almost empty parking lot.

Gladys, always helpful and cooperative, pranced herself to the entrance, while Paige juggled the gift bag and the creemees.

Faith was off today, but Paige checked in with Penny, who confirmed Hazel could indeed have the ice cream treat. The sweet nurse helped by taking Gladys's leash after kneeling down to give her ears a massage. They elected to take the outdoor pathway to Hazel's building so as not to get the hopes up of the residents in the assisted living area who would want Gladys to stop and visit with them.

"We can come back and visit when we're done with

TAMMY L. GRACE

Hazel. I just don't want this ice cream to melt." Paige followed as Gladys paraded into the main entrance and Penny led them to Hazel's room.

Hazel was sitting in her bed, as she had been on Thursday.

Her eyes brightened and a smile filled her face when she turned and saw them. "It's wonderful to see you again," she said, extending her hand to reach Gladys's snout. "It's not Thursday already, is it?"

Paige laughed. "No, it's Sunday and my day off. We brought you some treats." Paige set the gift bag in the chair and dug out one of the creemees from the bag. "I thought you could use a maple creemee."

Hazel's eyes widened and she reached for the container. "Oh, this is the best surprise." She took the spoon Paige handed her and let her remove the lid. "I haven't had one of these in months." She took a bite and moaned. "Delicious."

Paige transferred the gift bag to Hazel's tray and slid into the chair, digging into her own creemee. "Mmm, these are the best." Gladys watched the two of them and pawed at the top of the bed. "Do you want to get up there and snuggle with Hazel?"

Hazel nodded as she swallowed another bite of the creamy dessert. "There's plenty of room. She can curl up right here and keep me warm. I'm always chilled no matter how many blankets I have." She pointed at the spot next to her legs.

"Faith told me it was okay to allow her on the beds as long as you're okay with it."

"Oh, yes. I'd love nothing more." Hazel reached out to pet her head as Paige lifted her hindquarters and positioned her so she wasn't on top of Hazel.

Paige turned her attention to the bag. "I also picked out a few books I thought you might enjoy. Large print. I wasn't sure, so don't take offense."

Hazel nodded and she admired the bag. "You are as lovely as your mother. That is so kind of you. Go ahead and unwrap them and we'll have a look."

Paige felt like Santa Claus as she revealed each novel and Hazel beamed, eager to have Paige read from the back of each one. New releases from Nicholas Sparks, Kristin Hannah, and Debbie Macomber were among the selections. "Oh, my," said Hazel. "I'm not sure where to begin. They all sound wonderful."

The two of them visited for hours while Gladys dozed, resting her head against Hazel. She was so easy to talk to that it was like talking to her mom.

Paige told her new friend about Danny's car accident and his horrific injuries that had kept him in the hospital for weeks. "Once he got transferred to the care center, he started to give up. The outlook was grim, but that turned off a switch in him and I watched him wither each day." Tears plopped onto her sweater. "I couldn't make him fight."

Hazel patted her hand. "Sometimes, dear, there is nothing more to fight. It's hard to explain, but when I got sick just over a year ago now, Robert researched all the best treatments and doctors. He took so much time off work and did everything he could possibly do to get

41

me to the best doctors." She dabbed a tissue to her eyes. "I understood before he did that this was the end of the path for me. I fought because he needed me to, but I just couldn't do it any more. He finally understood that in these past few months. As for me, I'm convinced the good Lord knows what He is doing, and I'm ready to go when He calls me."

Paige pulled more tissues from the box. "Some days I'm glad Mom didn't suffer like Danny and just went to sleep. Other days, I wish I could have said goodbye. I didn't have time to learn everything I needed from her. Or my dad. I guess I didn't make the most of them when I had them."

Hazel nodded. "It's never enough, no matter how long we have them. Just remember, like I tell my Robert, listen to your heart and you'll hear your mom. You'll see her in the gorgeous spring flowers or the clear running water of the falls in the summer. Or even like now in the brilliant-colored leaves everywhere you look. Even in the first big snowfall, when everything is blanketed in calmness, she'll be there, Paige. She'll never leave you. A part of her will always be in you." She brought her hand to her chest. "Right here."

Hazel sighed and rested her head against her pillow. "I've learned you have to live life, find joy, do good, and treasure your friends and family. Take a few chances and step out of your comfort zone. Love deeply and do what you know is right. I finally convinced Robert to let me stay here and be happy for me because it's what *I* want. That's another of life's little nuggets. You do have to do what makes you happy. Robert has realized I'm at peace here, which I hope gives him some comfort. I don't want him to feel guilty. He's a wonderful son. I've tried to explain to him that I'm cherishing these last days, but I'm not clinging to life. I'm just living it, and when I slip away from this one, I know where I'm going. I'm not afraid."

Paige bobbed her head but couldn't speak.

Gladys moved closer to the edge of the bed and touched her paw to Paige's arm.

It brought a smile to her face and she bent down and kissed the top of her head. "You're such a sweet girl and know just when I need you, don't you?"

That prompted Gladys to get off the bed and sit next to the chair.

With both of their cheeks wet with tears, Hazel fingered the books and settled on the new Debbie Macomber for her first read. Paige offered to start reading it to her, and before she was done with the first chapter, Hazel's eyes closed.

Paige put the book away, making sure it was within easy reach, and led Gladys out of the room, both of them taking slow steps so as not to wake Hazel.

In the hall, she checked her watch and was surprised at how late it was but made a quick trip into the main building. Gladys needed to visit with her friends who would no doubt miss her if they didn't make the effort to stop inside.

When dinner was announced, she was able to pull Gladys away, and amid well wishes and lots of waving, they made their exit, promising to see everyone on Thursday.

Paige made the turn onto the highway and glanced in the rearview mirror, chuckling at the smile on Gladys's face and the happy glow in her eyes.

Spending time at a care center was the last thing she expected to bring a dog joy, but like Gladys, Paige found herself content and glad that she had made the trip.

CHAPTER 5

On Monday, the Winey Widows arrived with plenty of wine and snacks. They encouraged Paige to join their meeting. Technically, she qualified, but she wasn't sure about it.

It didn't take them long to convince her to at least stay and have a nibble. Before Paige knew it, she had spent three hours listening to their antics, laughing almost the whole time.

Now, she understood why her mother loved them so much. Rather than sit around moping about their widowhood, they met to focus on doing things that made them happy. They even had Jean on video chat so she could be part of the conversation. They were trying to figure out where to travel to this year for their annual trip.

They grumbled about the horrible stomach viruses one could catch and the ships stuck out in the ocean for days, so cruises were vetoed.

They all complained about each other's driving, so long road trips were out.

After a lengthy back-and-forth of ideas that would work for plane or train travel, they elected to each put a piece of paper in a bowl with a suggestion on where to go and have Paige draw the winning destination.

Paige stuck her hand into the bowl.

"Ireland," she announced, brows raised high.

Would these ladies really go so far?

"Oh, how exciting," said Agnes.

Norma, a natural organizer, was already scribbling notes on her pad, asking everyone about dates.

Paige chuckled at their excitement and went to make another cup of tea.

"You're welcome to join us," said Norma. "It looks like May works best."

"Oh, I don't know about that. I'd have to think about it and figure out who could watch over the store. Plus, I have Gladys."

"Jed can take Gladys, and if you can't find someone to man the store, just close it for a couple of weeks," suggested Cecilia.

Hazel's words about stepping out of her comfort zone and finding joy echoed in Paige's mind as she considered the offer. She had always wanted to travel, and ironically, Ireland was high on her list. She would love to sketch some of the old architecture and soak in the countryside. Not to mention, they could probably use someone a little younger to help them on a big trip like that.

She grinned, thinking back to her mom talking about Cecilia and Agnes befriending anyone they met on their travels and their ability to always find some strong men to help carry their bags.

Paige decided to take a chance.

"Okay, put me down for a yes, and I'll figure it out."

The group, including Jean on video, clapped at her decision. Then the chatter intensified as they all started shouting out places they wanted to see or stay.

Paige stayed out of that part of it. She didn't care where they slept or went—just the idea of such a trip was marvelous. She'd relish in the excitement and work on the practical matters later.

This would be her first big adventure on her own, but like Hazel had reminded her, Margot would always be with her and going with her friends would make it all the sweeter.

>))))

BEING the early part of October, it was prime leaf-peeping season, and Paige was so busy she missed lunch most days. On top of the influx of customers, she got frequent deliveries of books and gift items for the holidays. She ended up working nights to unbox, check it in, and get the products into the inventory system.

Jed stopped by for dinner each night, bringing along Bentley for a short visit, but never stayed long. It was also his busiest time of the year and he put in long days.

Thursday, Paige woke up excited to make the trip out to the center and took two audiobooks she thought Hazel might like. Both were wonderful stories about the connections we have with dogs, written by a new author Paige had discovered, Casey Wilson.

She found a compact disc player in the drawer and bundled it with the audiobooks, plus a new Christmas book that had just arrived, a soft scarf the color of washed denim, and added a few of her favorite teas to a tin.

At the center, she and Gladys found Faith straight-away and spent some time with everyone in the great room. After over an hour of visiting and plenty of belly rubs for Gladys, they walked over to Hazel's room.

Hazel was staring at the door and smiled when they walked through it.

"Oh, I've been waiting for you. Those books were wonderful. I finished all of them."

"Oh, wow. You are a fast reader."

She grinned and nodded at the television. "I'm not much for TV and there's not much else to do, so escaping into the pages of these lovelies was the best part of my week."

"I'll be sure and bring you some more on Sunday. I thought you might want to try a couple audiobooks, and I brought you a player you can borrow to listen to them." She set it up and showed her the buttons to use and then inserted the first disc.

Hazel's thin eyebrows rose. "Oh, that's nifty. The only downfall is I'll probably doze off while listening."

Paige showed her the button to use to back up the recording. "You can just go back to where you remember if you do fall asleep. Super easy and then you won't have to strain your eyes or hold the book."

"I like that idea. My eyes are worn out, but I just couldn't help myself."

Paige reached into the bag and showed her the scarf, gently placing it around her shoulders. "I thought that might help keep you warm and it matches your eyes."

She set the tin of tea on the bedside table. "I also brought you some yummy teas to try."

Hazel ran her hands over the soft yarn of the scarf. "This is just gorgeous and so cozy. I love it." She pulled it closer around her neck. "That tea looks wonderful. Brew us a couple of cups and we'll have it while we visit, and then maybe you can start reading that new Christmas book." Her eyes drifted to the book Paige had set next to her on the chair.

Paige situated Gladys on top of the bed and reminded her to stay, not that she needed to, since the dog knew more about what went on at Aspen Grove than she did. She wandered out to the common area and filled two cups with hot water, snapping on the lids.

The tea, an Earl Grey blend with a hint of vanilla and caramel, along with the classic lemony bergamot, met with Hazel's approval. Paige told her about the upcoming trip to Ireland with her mom's friends and how busy her week had been at the store.

"Oh, I think your mom would love the idea of you going with her group. I never traveled much and wish I would have. Home, here in Vermont, has always been my favorite place to be. The Harvest Festival is coming up at the end of the month. That was always one of my favorite outings. Those apple cider donuts are the best. Are you going?"

Paige shrugged. "I haven't even thought about it. It's hard to think too far ahead right now. That's what worried me about saying I would go to Ireland. I'm trying to approach life more like Gladys and live in the moment." She laughed and caressed the dog behind her ears.

"That's wise. It's easy to get caught up worrying too much about the future or regretting the losses of the past. I try to do the same and find something good about each day and focus on that."

Paige reached for the book and noticed her teacup was almost empty.

Hazel still had plenty. "I'll be right back. I need more hot water."

She was back in a few minutes and Hazel held up her finger. "I forgot to mention, Robert called me last Sunday night after you left." When she said his name, her eyes twinkled. "I let him know you and Gladys were coming to see me and he was so happy. He was worried I'd be lonely and is relieved to know I've made two new friends and that you're connected to the bookstore. He's taken so much time off, he won't be able to get away until the next holiday, but I so wish you could meet him."

"He sounds like a great guy and a terrific son. I'm glad he's not as worried about you now. This really is a lovely place."

"I've tried to tell him. They do a great job, and the nurses and aides are so friendly and attentive. If I was healthier and able to get around, I could stay in the other building. I think Robert would have been fine with that. Much like you said about your husband, when you get here, you know you're close to the grand finale, and that's not always easy to accept."

"You are such a strong person, Hazel. I admire your courage. I wish I was brave."

Hazel reached for her hand. "You're stronger and braver than you think."

THE DAYS PASSED with Paige adjusting to her new normal, handling things at the store while making sure all the normal household chores were handled.

Jed, like their dad, was a master of maintenance and fixing things, so she didn't have to worry about who would plow the snow or supply the firewood. He made sure everything was winterized.

She hadn't spent much time in her mother's room since she had passed away but wandered into it on Saturday night, longing to be close to her again.

From the window, Paige gazed at the tree, imagining her mom doing the same while admiring the glow of the warm lights and the bustle of people in the square. She glanced at the dresser with photos across the top, along with the baubles she had kept.

She ran her fingers across the stack of books on the nightstand. The familiar titles brought her comfort.

Paige was exhausted and eased onto the bed, resting her head against her mother's pillow. Gladys jumped right up on the bed, as she had always slept next to Margot.

Someone, during the four days she had spent in her room, she wasn't sure who but suspected one of her mother's friends, had changed the bedding and straightened Margot's room, so it was all clean and fresh, but if Paige shut her eyes and sniffed at the pillow, she smelled her mom. The hint of perfume she wore, the rose soap she always used, it lingered there, embedded in the fibers.

Paige thought she had been holding up well enough these last few weeks, keeping busy, visiting with customers and Hazel, then falling into bed exhausted at the end of the day. Her fatigue should have guaranteed that she would sleep, but the salty taste of tears still trickled across her lips, as it did now.

She eyed the walk-in closet and chastised herself for the waiting clutter of her mother's clothes and things. She just couldn't bring herself to go through and sort them yet. She was still playing the fantasy in her mind that her mom was on a trip and would return.

She wasn't crazy; she knew it wasn't true, but it gave her a reprieve.

She wasn't strong enough to face it all yet.

Paige still needed her mom and suspected, like Hazel had said, no matter how long she would have lived, it wouldn't have been long enough. The person who she always relied on to get her through the toughest things wasn't here to hold her this time—wasn't there to tell her everything would be okay.

She pulled the quilt up from the bottom of the bed and snuggled under it.

Gladys inched closer and she felt her hot breath on her neck.

She felt as she had when she was a little girl and got to sleep with her parents—warm and safe. She needed that tonight.

Instead of getting up to go to her own room, Paige nestled further under the quilt that had been on her mom's bed for years. With one more look out the window where she could see the highest branches of the Wishing Tree twinkling, she shut her eyes.

CHAPTER 6

Sunday, Paige and Gladys stopped by Cobblestone and picked up a few of the apple cider donuts for Hazel. The bakery only had them in the fall, and she wanted to make sure Hazel got a chance to enjoy them.

Hazel wouldn't be able to attend the festival, where hordes of tourists and locals alike would keep the bakery and the extra food trucks that serviced the festival busy.

Gladys took her appointed position next to Hazel while Paige rounded up some napkins and paper plates. Over tea and donuts, Hazel's sweet smile and stories were cheering. Paige missed the wisdom of her mother and the calmness she instilled, just in her presence. She had made her feel safe, even when her world was broken.

Sitting with Hazel and listening to her talk had the same effect.

There was something about the older generation that Paige had always found comforting. She couldn't put her finger on it but thought it might be their confidence and fearlessness in the future that she found inspiring. They had lived through tough times, experienced loss and suffering, and still were convinced the sun would rise tomorrow.

Paige's mom was like that. Too busy living life to worry. And now her friends were making big plans for the future. Instead of wondering if they'd be able to go on a trip, they assumed they would.

As precarious as Hazel's situation was, even she looked for the happiness in each day with no fear of the future.

Their resolve amazed Paige. She was still shaky and unbalanced from the unexpected death of her mom when she wasn't yet over losing Danny. She thought about how much worse she would have felt had she stayed in Albany and not had the last four months with her mom.

Hazel was right. She needed to seek out the happiness in her life and relish it.

She read several chapters of the sweet holiday story about second chances and little coincidences that bring two old friends together.

Hazel sighed when Paige closed the cover. "What a lovely story." She adjusted her bed and closed her eyes. "It reminds me of my biggest regret. I don't have many, but one in particular has been poking at me lately."

She went on to tell Paige about a man, a friend she

had known from her youth who visited her town not long after she lost her husband. He was sweet on her when they were in school but after he joined the military, she hadn't kept up with him. He'd made a point of returning to their small hometown and reaching out to her.

"He more than hinted that he still had feelings for me and would be happy to wait until I was ready but wanted me to know he had always loved me." She exhaled and fiddled with her scarf, her eyes still closed.

"I was too worried about what others would think and how it might hurt Robert. I should have followed my heart and made a new life with him, but I didn't. I let him slip away and wasn't very nice about it at the time. I've always been sorry for that. Especially now, as I look back on these last years, when I was all alone after my son left. I could have had a partner, someone to share my life with, someone to hold my hand each night. I regret that, especially now, in the winter of my life."

She opened her eyes. "Paige, listen to me. If you get a second chance at love, don't squander it. Be smarter than I was and don't let it slip through your fingers. Grab on to it with all you have."

It was getting late and they would soon be serving dinner.

Paige helped Gladys off the bed and started to gather her things.

As she straightened the books on the bedside table, Hazel reached out a hand, grabbing hold of Paige's wrist. "I can never thank you enough for spending your free time with me. I'm sure you have much better things to do than listen to an old lady ramble on about the past, but I do love that you come to see me." She glanced down at Gladys. "Not to mention, letting me cuddle with this sweet girl."

Gladys wagged her tail happily, taking in the compliment.

Tears filled Paige's eyes as she gripped the woman's bony hand in hers. "Don't say that, Hazel. You're the highlight of my week. I was afraid to come here and did it because I felt a duty to honor my mom, but now I can't imagine *not* visiting you. I think you've done more for me than I've done for you."

Before she knew it, she bent forward and kissed Hazel's soft cheek. "You get some rest, and we'll see you Thursday." Despite Paige suspecting Hazel was already dozing, she smiled and squeezed her hand.

MONDAY WHEN AGNES, Cecilia, and Norma arrived for their meeting, they came laden with takeout bags that Paige recognized from the Crooked Porch, and the delicious aroma made her instantly hungry.

Over tender brisket, a crispy cabbage salad, and the best truffle mac and cheese she had tasted, the four of them visited, and Norma caught them up on options for Ireland. Jean was on video and kept asking them to focus the camera on the food so she could see what she was missing.

As Paige listened to their banter, she had an inkling they enjoyed the anticipation of planning their outing perhaps even more than the actual trip. They wanted to stay in the countryside but didn't want to drive, especially on the wrong side of the road, so were looking for small tour groups.

Once they had exhausted their discussion of tours and lodging options, Cecilia refilled all their wine-glasses and met Paige's eyes. "So, are you working on any illustrations at the moment, dear?"

Paige shook her head. "No. I cancelled or delayed all my contracts. I haven't even picked up a pencil to sketch anything since Danny's accident. I had decided to start getting back in touch with my publishing and author contacts, but then Mom…"

Norma waved her hand around the space. "I'm sure you're plenty busy with the bookstore now. Do you think you'll have time to go back to your art? Maybe you'll have to get some help here."

Paige shrugged. "I've just been avoiding the decision. I love drawing and it's always been my fun little world, but since the accident, I just can't get motivated. Mom tried to encourage me, reminding me how slow winters are around here and that I needed to get some work lined up. Now, like you say, I barely have a spare minute."

Cecilia patted her arm. "You just have to take a day at a time and do what feels right. There are no rules about how you tackle things or how you should feel. We all know the bookstore was your mom's happy place, but it might not be yours. You need to do what brings *you* joy. Like Norma said, you might have to find some help to give you time to do that."

Paige brought the wineglass to her lips, not really wanting more but needing a moment. "I haven't even tackled going through Mom's things. It's all too much. I'm not sure what to do. Keeping the store going sort of gives me a built-in purpose, one I don't have to think about, just keep doing." Tears plopped onto her jeans. "It sounds crazy, but I tell myself Mom is just gone, and she'll be back soon."

They all nodded. "No, that doesn't sound crazy," said Cecilia. "We've all been there and played those little games. You have to do whatever keeps you sane. Trust me, we understand."

Norma bobbed her head. "Your mom, more than anything, would want you to be happy and fulfilled. She loved you and Jed so much and would not want the store to be a burden or for you to feel tied to it. As much as she loved it, she loved you more. You should take your time and the answer will come to you, Paige. Sometimes, when you quit thinking and worrying and let your brain take a vacation, that's when it hits you."

Jean piped up from the screen on the tablet they had placed on the table. "I agree. Try to relax and let things evolve naturally. Once the fall leaves are done, you won't be near as swamped, but then you'll have the holiday events. Margot poured everything into the store, but she didn't have other interests like you do, so don't think anyone will judge you if you need some help. Just ask. We're always full of advice if nothing else."

That brought a round of healthy laughter and cries for dessert and coffee.

Agnes was happy to polish off the rest of Paige's wine, and while they nibbled on cookies from the stash in Margot's freezer, the women chatted about local happenings.

Paige wouldn't use the word gossipy, but they all had an inquisitive streak, much like Gladys. They liked to know what was going on in Linden Falls and who was involved in all of it.

As she listened to them, she realized in addition to the wisdom they imparted, part of what gave her comfort was the protection they offered. With her mom gone, that buffer that she never thought about, the one between her and mortality, was gone. Having her mom's friends around made her feel less vulnerable.

Paige chuckled as she saw the last one out and locked the door, then trudged upstairs to bed. She had long since given up on trying to make Gladys sleep on the floor and had become accustomed to feeling the warmth of her body against her legs.

That made her think of Hazel and she whispered a quick prayer for her.

IN THE LITTLE spare time she had over the next couple of days, Paige gave some thought to the idea of getting back to her art. Until this past year, it had always brought her joy. Maybe it could be her refuge once again.

Thursday, she slept in, having stayed up late Wednesday evening to get caught up on receiving and spent some time perusing the shelves, looking for more books Hazel might enjoy.

After a quick shower and a cup of tea, she and Gladys set out for Aspen Grove.

Faith met them at the front door and asked her to come to her office for a few minutes before heading to visit with the residents. Faith pointed to a comfy-looking couch and sat next to Paige, resting a hand on top of Gladys's head.

"There's no easy way to tell you this, but Hazel passed away early this morning. I'm so very sorry, Paige."

The happiness Paige had felt when she came through the door evaporated and a lump formed in her throat. She shook her head. "But she was fine on Thursday."

Faith nodded, her blue eyes full of compassion. "I know, but she slipped away in her sleep last night. I want you to know, she didn't suffer."

Paige couldn't control the tears that quickly escalated to sobs.

Gladys placed a paw on the top of her knee, looking at her with confusion.

She reached a hand to the dog. "Oh, this is just too much."

Faith's door opened and an aide brought in a tray with steaming cups of tea.

Faith took them both and then urged Paige to sip it. "I've called her son, Robert. He's making all the arrangements. He's also hoping you'll come. He'd like to meet you and thank you for spending time with her."

Paige couldn't speak as the now silent tears rolled down her cheeks. She blew out a breath. "I don't know if I can do another funeral so soon." Her hands shook as she brought the cup to her lips and swallowed a sip. "How do you do this? You must have lost so many people that have lived here. People you've come to care for."

"Oh, yes, too many to count." Her eyes glinted, but she smiled. "It's not easy, but over the years I've learned to focus on what I can do and the difference I can make for them while they're here. I work hard to treat my patients with dignity and respect. I get to know them and spend time with them. I love to make them smile, and while some of them are tougher than others in that regard, I don't ever give up."

Paige took several tissues from the box Faith offered. "I was just getting to know her. I really enjoyed spending time with her. It's just not fair."

"I agree. It's not fair. Hazel was a sweetheart and an easy patient to love. She was also at peace with her situation. We talked several times, and she wasn't afraid. Not that she was happy about her situation, but she had accepted it. She had a strong faith and knew she would see her family members again. Just yesterday we were talking, and she told me she had the most vivid dream about her mother and her husband. She smiled as she described it, almost as if she knew it wouldn't be much longer before she saw them again."

Paige took another long swallow of the warm liquid. "Do you think she knew?"

Faith smiled. "I think she might have. I've seen it before, and the situations are always similar, a vision where the patient believes her family members are there or such a lifelike dream that it feels like it was real. Many times, death comes shortly after such an experience."

"Like they're being reunited or ushered to heaven, you think?"

She shrugged. "I like to think so. When you're ready, I know the residents are excited to see Gladys, but usually we take her to the room of the latest to depart, and we let her smell and see they are gone. I'm not certain, but it seems like it helps her understand, and she'll accept that Hazel has left us."

Paige sucked in her breath. "I'm not sure I'm up to it."

"I know it's hard. I can take Gladys if you'd rather not. I understand how difficult this is, and it's amplified because you lost your mom so recently. Often the first loss after a significant one, like that of your mom, can bring all those feelings up and cause intense feelings of grief."

"Just give me a few minutes."

"No problem. I've got some things to check on and I'll be back in a few." Faith gave Gladys a scratch behind her ears before leaving.

Gladys rested her head in Paige's lap, and Paige ran her hand over her head, letting the dog soak up her sadness and ease her heavy heart. With every stroke of her hand, Paige felt her pulse slow.

Logically, she'd known Hazel wasn't long for this world, but she hadn't expected her to be gone so quickly. She had planned to be able to spend many months with her, reading books and sipping tea.

It wasn't the same as losing her mother, but that sense of unfinished conversations and wanting more time was the same. Life was tenuous and more fragile than she'd ever thought. This year had been nothing but loss after loss and she was exhausted. She didn't want to let Faith down, or all the smiling people down the hallway, but she wasn't sure she could keep coming here. How many more people would she just get to know, to have them disappear?

She looked into the soulful brown eyes staring at hers and bowed her head to meet Gladys. "How do you do it, Gladys? How are you able to keep up your sweet disposition and make everyone smile, knowing they might not be here next time?"

Gladys thumped her tail against the floor and moved her snout deeper into Paige's lap. She couldn't deny the residents interaction with Gladys—they loved her, and she brought them joy and let them forget their worries for a short time. She also couldn't disappoint her mom. She had been able to handle it and had come here for years. Paige needed to buck up and stiffen her spine. Like her mom had always told her, she needed to concentrate on what she could do.

Faith opened the door and raised her brows. "Well?"

"Let's go make the rounds and, like you said, go by Hazel's room and let Gladys give her a proper goodbye."

The nurse embraced her in a tight hug, rocking her back and forth. "I'm so glad. We need you both here. You make a big difference."

Faith led the way to the common room, and for almost an hour, they moved from person to person, where Gladys delivered her signature wag and lit up their faces with smiles. Faith collected them in time to get them to the other building before Paige had to leave to open the store.

With each step Paige took toward the room at the end of the hall, dread weighed on her. Each move forward felt like she was pulling her foot out of quicksand. Ahead, Faith stopped at the door, waiting for them to catch up.

Paige finally stepped inside, with Gladys beside her.

They went to Hazel's empty bed, the scent of her lotion lingering.

Glancing at the other bed in the room, she saw supplies had been placed on the tray and table. "Florence" was written on the patient information whiteboard on the wall.

She pointed at it. "Hazel would have enjoyed having a roommate. Too bad Florence didn't arrive sooner." Gladys was busy sniffing at the sheets and blankets, paying particular attention to the pillow.

Next to the beautiful pink rose bouquet that must have been delivered earlier in the week were the books, scarf, and disc player, all in a neat stack.

"Be sure and take your things," Faith said, moving to gather them together.

She handed them to Paige, who placed the books on Florence's table. "Maybe she'll enjoy the books. I'll stop in and see her next time."

Paige brought the scarf to her nose and inhaled. Tears filled her eyes as the scent of lavender reminded her of Hazel. She wrapped it around her neck and took hold of Gladys's leash. "Let's go, girl. Hazel is in heaven with Mom."

CHAPTER 7

*P*aige got through the next few days with almost no memory of any of it—her words and movements automatic and without thought.

Everything in her wanted to curl up in bed and hide from the world, but the store was much too busy to close, so she simply went through the motions.

She smiled like an actress in a role as she helped the customers. And she made the daily deposits, packed up online orders, and put out more stock—all the while pushing her grief to the back of her mind.

Gladys must have sensed her sadness, and for the first time since Paige had reopened the store, the dog didn't wander down the street to visit or spend part of the day with Bentley and Jed.

Instead, she sat at Paige's feet or near the fire all day, never letting her out of sight.

On Saturday, Paige woke to a craving for an almond

croissant. She walked over to Cobblestone before the bookstore opened to grab one of the decadent treats to go with her tea. Her eyes blurred with tears when she saw the tray of apple cider donuts, but escaped before they fell and embarrassed her.

Thankfully, she had lost her muffin top after Danny's accident but had also shed twenty extra pounds in the process. She hadn't indulged in bakery treats until returning to Linden Falls, where they were just a few footsteps down the street.

She vowed to eat healthier as soon as the season was over and things settled down.

She sure didn't need one more thing to feel guilty about right now.

Back at the bookstore, she settled into her favorite chair and nibbled on her breakfast, sipping some Earl Grey before the first customers arrived. She had just finished the last bite when the bells on the door jingled and a tall man stepped inside, his eyes scanning the space.

He noticed her and smiled. "You blend in like part of the décor." He glanced at Gladys. "Oh, and you've even got a sweet friend."

He stepped closer and Paige squinted.

Something about his voice was familiar.

As he got closer, her eyes widened when she recognized the smile underneath the dark scruff of a beard. "Reed?" She put the book down and stood.

He grinned and wrapped her in a warm hug. "Paige,

I can't believe you're here." He released her and stood, still smiling, with his hands on her shoulders. "When the people out at Aspen Grove mentioned a bookstore and Paige, I just knew I had to come and see for myself."

She frowned, studying his deep blue eyes. Eyes she hadn't seen since they both left Linden Falls for college over three decades ago. Not being one for high school reunions, she had never kept in close touch with any classmates. "Aspen Grove?"

"My mom." Some of the light faded in his eyes. "She had to go in just this past week."

She gasped. "Florence? I was out there on Thursday morning and saw they were getting ready for a new patient."

He nodded. "Yeah, not what I had planned, but here we are. Thank you for leaving that nice selection of books for her."

She motioned him to the counter, where there was a spare chair next to hers behind the desk. "Come sit down and tell me more." She added water to the kettle and brewed two more cups of tea while he hung his coat and petted Gladys.

"What a sweet dog," he said as he massaged the side of her face.

"That's Gladys. She's a bit of a busybody, so my mom thought that name fit her." She smiled and handed him a cup. She slipped into her chair and added her mom's wrap around her shoulders. Over tea and between a few customers, she explained she found herself back in Linden Falls after losing her husband, and then with her mom passing unexpectedly just a few weeks ago, she had taken over running the bookstore.

He hung his head. "I'm so sorry about your mom. She was such a sweetheart of a lady. I remember her coming to our classes and reading to us when we were little. She always brought everyone a book." He swallowed another sip from his cup. "Oh, gosh, I'm sorry about your husband as well. I only knew your mom and have such fond memories of her."

His eyes swept over the store again. "Of this place. Your whole family."

"Jed's running the hardware store now. You'll have to stop by and say hello."

"I'll do that. Maybe we could all get together for dinner or something?"

She nodded before getting up to ring up a sale. "So what's going on with your mom? How long are you in town for?"

He raised his brows. "She fell and broke her hip. Just had surgery and now she can't really get around. She needs help, plus physical therapy. She had moved out of Linden Falls years ago over to Potter Creek, but this is the closest care center and it's wonderful, so she was glad to get in. I tried to convince her to come to New York, but she wouldn't hear of it."

"Wow, so you just picked up and moved?"

"Basically. I sublet my apartment and I can work

from anywhere. I'm staying over at the Wishing Tree Inn right now. Speaking of that, I visited with Neva. I can't believe she's still around. She was talking my ear off, telling me all about the Wishing Tree and showing me her binders of wishes. Wow."

"I know. She has made that her life's mission. She never married and has always been alone. She's a little different but was always sweet to mom, and they both shared a love for that tree. I used to believe but am old enough to know better now."

"It's a stunning tree. I noticed those drawings of yours on the wall. You ought to do those on cards and sell them. I bet they'd go like hotcakes."

"Hmm. That's actually a good idea. I might make that my first project, just to get back in the groove. I haven't done much drawing since Danny. So, you're just going to stay at the inn?"

He shrugged. "Until I can find a place to rent. I figured I'll stay here until Mom's up to being able to get around and can go home. I can't stand the thought of leaving her without being able to check on her each day, you know?"

He was just as kind as she remembered. "What about your sister? Is she nearby?"

He shook his head. "No, Lynn is all the way out in California and still has kids at home. It's easy for me. Like I said, I can work from anywhere."

"What do you do?"

He grinned and tipped his head in the direction of the shelves. "I'm a writer, a novelist."

"Oh, my gosh. How did I not know that? I do, well, I did freelance illustrating for children's books."

"Oh, you always were so talented. That's wonderful. I wonder if Mom knows that. I write under a pen name, so it's like being in witness protection." He laughed. "The good thing is, I don't have to do any public appearances. My publisher thinks it builds the intrigue and gets more sales because nobody really knows who writes these books."

"How many books have you published?"

He looked up, thinking. "I believe this next one is my fifty-first."

Her mouth dropped open. "Okay, I have to know." She gritted her teeth and wrinkled her nose. "Can you tell me your pen name?"

He held up his hands. "Sorry, I'm sworn to secrecy. It's in my contract."

She frowned and stuck out her lip. "You can trust me."

He shook his head. "No doubt, but let's hear more about your illustrations. Show me some of your books."

Gladys followed Paige to the children's section and stood at the door, her signal that she wanted to take her usual walk.

Paige opened the door and the dog scooted out, heading across the square. She watched as she stopped at the gazebo and got a few pats and some petting from people sitting on the benches, then walked toward the hardware store with Calvin from the newspaper.

The dog's gait quickened when she joined him, a little skip of joy obvious.

Gladys often sought him out, and the sight of them walking together always made Paige giggle. Those two were kindred spirits, with him being on the lookout for newsworthy items and poking his nose into any rumors he heard. Gladys being a natural busybody made them a good team.

With her arms full of books from the shelf her mother had so lovingly labeled with her daughter as the illustrator, Paige returned to the counter.

"Mom carried them all and always had to tell anyone who walked through the door."

That had always embarrassed Paige, but now the memory made her smile.

He thumbed through them, praising her work. "I'm not in the children's book world, so I never knew. These are fabulous. You'll have to go and visit Mom and tell her all about it. She'll be so proud."

"She inspired my love of drawing, that's for sure. She was the best art teacher."

More customers arrived and interrupted their conversation, and Reed jumped right in, offering to bag things, and even helped customers with recommendations for books they might enjoy. He was well versed in all genres, making it hard for Paige to figure out what he wrote.

Her first thought was thrillers or suspense, something like Lee Child. He seemed to know all about that genre, but he also steered a few ladies toward popular women's fiction and romance titles.

Like most writers, Reed was probably an avid reader. He was going to keep her guessing, that was for sure. The hours flew by as they visited and waited on customers.

In the early afternoon, Reed looked at his watch. "I should probably run and check on Mom. Do you want to call Jed and see if he can meet for dinner? We could get caught up with each other. We could meet up at Woody's if it's still in business?"

"Sure, Woody's sounds perfect. Jed will be happy. He loves pizza. Let's say six thirty. Tell your mom hello and Gladys and I are due out there tomorrow, so I'll be sure to stop in and visit with her."

"Sounds great." He pulled out his cell phone. "Shall we trade digits, as the kids say?"

If someone else had asked her that, it would've been weird and awkward. But with Reed, she laughed and retrieved her phone from the counter.

As she lounged in bed on Sunday morning, she smiled. The night before had been the best night she'd had since her mom died. It was fun to leave her sadness behind for a while and just visit with Reed to reminisce about old times. He and Jed had been good friends growing up, and Reed had always spent time at their house, as Jed had at his.

Jed offered to let Reed stay with him until he could find a rental. He had plenty of room and it was just him and Bentley. Reed didn't want to impose but, after much discussion and assurance, by the end of the night had agreed to take him up on his offer.

A ripple of excitement fluttered in Paige's chest. She'd always had a bit of a crush on Reed, in that way a little sister is in awe of her older brother's friends, especially the cute ones that are sweet. She doubted he ever knew it, as it was all a teenage girl's fantasies, but seeing him again brought back those same feelings of attraction.

She glanced at her nightstand and saw the photo she kept of her and Danny, and she was mortified. How could she even think those things with Danny barely being gone?

Paige pulled the pillow over her face.

Silently, she berated herself for noticing how handsome Reed was, even with the little wisps of gray near his ears and the same flecks in his beard.

To think of it, her own roots were getting gray, and she hadn't kept her last appointment for a cut and color. The expanding line of silver along her part needed some attention. Like Margot, she had dark hair. While she had thought the silver strands in her mom's hair looked elegant, she wasn't quite ready to embrace them herself.

She felt heat rush up her neck and fill her cheeks. Of all the times over the last thirty years, she would have to run into Reed when she was weeks overdue for a touch-up.

When he'd hugged her goodbye the night before, she'd closed her eyes and savored the scent of cedarwood along his collar. She'd inhaled deeper and hints of clove mixed with the woodsy scent made her want to stay there forever.

His arms had wrapped her in a firm embrace and he'd held her longer than a quick farewell. Nobody had hugged her like that since Danny. The feelings that bubbled to the surface surprised her, but she couldn't deny how safe she felt with him.

Danny had been her everything, but they'd also had some rough years, especially during the miscarriages and loss of hope. They had recovered and become closer in many ways, sharing the disappointment and fashioning a life without children.

Her husband had been the major breadwinner with a great job, so she had been able to do her freelance work without worrying about making a living. All summer her mom had encouraged her to get back into it, but now, it was too much to think about. She couldn't face making all the calls to the people she had worked with and let down.

Reed's idea of making greeting cards did appeal to her, though. What was she thinking? She didn't have time for frivolity and had to focus on making a living and keeping the bookstore solvent.

She hadn't even had time to formulate a plan. She was too busy putting one foot in front of the other and doing what her mom would have done each day, trying to keep her memory alive and honor her. When she dug deeper and thought more about what she wanted to do, her mind became jumbled and she couldn't face those decisions. The store's revenue was on track for this time of year, and she needed to make the most of this busy time through the holidays. Things would slow down after the first of the year and she'd figure out what to do then.

Gladys still snoozed next to her, having stayed up late waiting for her.

"Wake up, sleepyhead," she said, making circles on the upturned belly. In the last weeks since they'd started sleeping together, Gladys had returned to her sleeping position of belly up, four legs in the air.

They were getting used to each other.

Gladys slowly opened her eyes, then stretched before jumping off the bed.

After a slow start, breakfast, and a couple of chores, they were finally ready to go out to Aspen Grove in the early afternoon.

Paige dreaded visiting Hazel's old room but was looking forward to seeing Reed's mom. She hadn't seen Mrs. Walker in years, probably since she'd come home to visit during her college years and run into her.

She pulled into a spot and Gladys perked up, swishing her tail as they walked to the main entrance. Penny was on duty today, so they checked in and headed to the skilled nursing building and down the hallway.

Paige peeked into the room.

Florence was in her bed, watching television, and Hazel's bed was still empty.

She politely knocked on the doorframe and smiled when Florence turned toward her. "Hey, Mrs. Walker."

The woman waved her hand and clicked off the television. "No need to be formal. Please call me Florence. Reed said you'd be stopping by and I'm so glad you did."

Paige pointed at the dog. "This is Gladys and she's a therapy dog. We've been coming out to visit the residents. Do you mind if she comes in your room?"

"Oh, heavens no. I'd love it." Rather than a hospital gown, Florence was wearing a sweatshirt and loose sweatpants. She was thinner than Paige remembered and seemed smaller, her back hunched across her shoulders. Freckles and age spots dotted her cheeks, and the dark hair Paige remembered was now pure white, cut in a short, no-nonsense style.

Florence scooted to the edge of the bed, gingerly, taking extra care of her right side. "What a gorgeous girl." She smiled as she ran her hands over Gladys's head.

Gladys responded with a rapid tail wag and a toothy smile.

"Reed is so grateful to Jed for offering him a place to stay. That's so kind of him. Truth be told, I'm glad he'll have some company. My son spends far too much time alone."

"The life of a writer, I suspect." Paige let go of the leash and slid into the chair next to Florence's bed.

"He also told me about you illustrating children's books. I looked up several of them and I just love them!" She pointed at the tablet on her bedside table. "I'm not surprised you found a way to use your talent." She winked and added, "Don't tell anyone, but you were my favorite student. And the most talented one."

Paige brought her hand to her chest. She was truly touched. "That's so sweet of you., Mrs. Wal—um... Florence. I give you the credit for helping me discover art and teaching me so much."

"Had I stayed in Linden Falls, I probably would have known all about you, but once Lynn graduated, we ended up moving over to Potter Creek and have been there ever since. I would have loved to stay here, but Reed's dad had a job offer he couldn't pass up, and it was easy to get a teaching job there."

Paige asked her how her hip was feeling and listened as Florence went through the litany of exercises she was doing and lamented the fact that she was exhausted most of the time. "I hate that this happened. There's nothing scarier at my age than a bad fall. The bright spot in all of it is getting to have Reed here. I know it would have been easier for him to find me a place in New York, but I don't want to be in the city."

They chatted more about art and their favorite mediums. "They said I could have my easel in here, so Reed's going to bring it and my paints for me, along with all my sketch pads and pencils. I'm going stir-crazy already and I'm supposed to be here for about six weeks. Wait—

I know. You should bring your sketch pad the next time you come. That would be fun, wouldn't it?"

The idea of working with Mrs. Walker—she would never get used to calling her Florence—sparked something inside Paige.

"That would be fantastic and the kick in the pants I need to get back into it. I've been struggling since my husband died. Now with Mom gone, I haven't been inspired." She smiled at the woman, whose kind eyes she had passed along to her son. "Until now."

Florence grinned. "I'd love nothing more. Shall we say next Sunday? No therapy on Sunday so I should be rested up."

"Perfect." Paige glanced at the table and scanned the titles of the stack of books, hoping to ferret out one that might be written by Reed. "If you need any reading material, let me know. I'm happy to bring you any books you want."

"That's kind of you, dear. It was so nice for you to leave those others for me. Reed is able to keep me well stocked through his publisher. They are constantly sending him advanced copies to read or new releases. He usually passes them on to me." She beamed with pride. "One of the perks of having a son who is an author."

"I don't suppose I can convince you to divulge his pen name?" Paige raised her brows and grinned. "You know I'm trustworthy."

Florence bent her head closer to Paige's with Gladys in the middle of them. "He warned me you might hound me for it. Sorry, dear, my lips are sealed."

Paige laughed at her clandestine whispering that provided her with zero information and shrugged. "I had to try."

CHAPTER 8

On Monday, Vera, who had been Margot's hairdresser and now did Paige's hair, had a cancellation and was able to get her in at the end of the day. That meant leaving the bookstore in the hands of Norma, who was happy to come a bit early for the Winey Widows and handle any sales.

After almost two hours in the chair, Paige admired her restored hair, now a shiny chestnut similar to her natural color, with a few deep copper and golden high-lights running through it, much like the leaves on her mother's beloved Wishing Tree.

She left the salon and headed back to the bookstore with a new spring in her step, her shoulder-length cut swinging with each step. The aroma wafting from the Crooked Porch Café led her to the door. She didn't feel like more leftovers and was craving one of their juicy burgers. She stepped inside and made her way to the small bar to place an order to go.

Paige did a double take when she noticed Reed sitting in one of the five chairs along the front of the bar.

He smiled at her, making her pulse quicken.

She smiled back, then studied his face and noticed how his wide grin reached all the way to the corners of his eyes, where tiny crinkles formed. His steely blue eyes glimmered with a bit of mystery. He'd always been an attractive guy, but age had only increased his appeal.

She saw his mouth moving and realized she hadn't heard a word he said. "Sorry, what?"

"I was just joking, saying you caught me. I've had a long day and decided to treat myself to dinner. You should join me." He pointed to the empty chair next to his.

She shook her head. "Oh, no. I was just going to get an order to go."

"Come on, don't make me eat alone." He stood and pulled the chair out for her.

She was powerless to resist.

He hung her coat on the back of the tall chair and took his seat after she was settled into hers. "I haven't ordered yet," he said.

"Oh, good. I'm in the mood for one of their cheeseburgers." Surprisingly, she really was. Her grief-stricken low appetite had vanished and left her stomach feeling hungry.

Nicole, the waitress who was always cheerful and had been so sweet to her mom, delivered their iced teas and offered to review the specials.

They both opted for cheeseburgers with homemade fries.

She took out her phone and tapped on the screen. "I better text Norma and let her know I'll be late and not to wait. She was watching the place while I got my haircut."

"Your hair looks great, by the way." He dipped his head in her direction. "Isn't it late for the store to be open anyway?"

"It's a long story. Norma, you remember her, our high school librarian?" He nodded. "Anyway, she and two other good friends of my mom's, Cecilia and Agnes, gather at the store every Monday night for their Winey Widows meeting. Mom was always a part of that group. Cecilia taught math when we were in high school, remember? They're a hoot and I left them in charge."

He shrugged. "Three retirees, a barrel of wine, and a bookstore…what could go wrong?" He grinned. "I can't picture Norma and Cecilia drinking wine at all. They seemed so prim and proper in school."

She raised her brows and laughed. "You'd be surprised. They've definitely mastered drinking wine. I think it's the years of practice." She took a long sip from her iced tea. "You mentioned you were busy today. What did you do?"

"Made the trip over to Mom's to get some of her things she wanted and get her mail forwarded, stuff like that." He sighed as he reached for a sugar packet. "Realistically, I'm not sure she'll ever go home. The house isn't designed for anyone in her shape. It's too big for her to take care of, and it would take quite a bit to remodel it to make it safe. I don't want her falling again and she really needs help. I'm trying to convince her to move into the assisted living part of the facility once she's recovered."

"I bet that's not going to be an easy task. When I saw her yesterday, she struck me as still being fairly independent."

He laughed and nodded. "That's a nice way of saying stubborn. I offered to move in with her when she gets out, but honestly, I'm not sure that would be great for either of us. Sometimes I forget to eat when I'm writing and go days without even looking outside. I would be a horrible caretaker. Not to mention that she likes to chat and I need it quiet when I'm working. It would be a disaster, but I wanted to at least give her that option."

Nicole slid a plate of fresh bread and dipping oil between them. "The kitchen is backed up a little, so you can snack on this while you wait."

He offered Paige the first piece and then took one of his own. "Let alone, she's not a real fan of having me help her with showering and personal care. It's awkward for both of us."

"I can understand that. That would make me feel vulnerable and weak if my son had to help me with personal care. I mean, if I had one."

"Yeah, I can't imagine having my daughter doing that for me, either."

Paige noticed that Reed hadn't said much about his personal life. He probably couldn't get a word in with all her dumping about Danny and then her mom. "How old is your daughter?"

"She's twenty-six and gorgeous. She's just graduated from medical school and snagged a residency at Mayo, so despite wanting to escape winters, she's stuck with snow." He took out his phone and scrolled to show her a few photos of Tessa, who was indeed stunning, with her dad's blue eyes and her face framed by dark blond hair.

"She's lovely. You must be so proud."

"Tessa's got me wrapped around her finger. Her mother and I divorced years ago. I missed out on so much of her life, but now as an adult, we've grown closer and see more of each other. She went to school in New York, which I loved. I got to experience all of that with her. Her mom moved to Florida and was hoping Tessa would go somewhere closer to her."

"That has to be hard for her mom," Paige said, thinking of how her own mother had anticipated every visit Paige could maneuver.

He dipped the last bite of his bread into the oil on his saucer. "It was. Willa, that's my ex-wife, she had a hard time being so removed from Tessa's life these last few years, but now she's remarried and is immersed in her own world. Her husband had kids and they live near them."

"I don't remember you dating anyone named Willa," Paige said.

"She was never around here. Willa was an editor with a prestigious publishing house but now is a freelancer. I met her by pitching a story idea to her at a big conference. She wanted to read my manuscript and we met a few times. She passed on it but connected me with other editors and really helped me get my start. One thing led to another and we became a couple, then married, and soon after, we had Tessa. Willa is a top-notch editor, but looking back, we should have never married."

"Mind if I ask why?" Paige said.

He took a slow drink from his glass before leaning back in his chair, a long sigh escaping. "Well, for my part, I think my excitement of having her help me with my book got tangled up with attraction, and it all sort of snowballed and took on a life of its own. Before I knew it, we were married. I was young and naïve. She's actually a little older than me, and I think she wanted a child so badly that it overshadowed her judgment."

Paige tore off a piece from her thick slice of bread. "Do you get along now?"

"Yes. It wasn't this way initially, but now we get along and cooperate when it comes to Tessa. Otherwise, we're more like colleagues. Sometimes we chat about the publishing world, but I only see her at big events, like Tessa's graduation."

Paige wondered if Tessa had her dad's personality.

He shoved the saucer to the other side of the bar. "Here I am rambling on, telling you more than you asked, and haven't given you time to share anything.

You mentioned you don't have a son, but what about other children?"

She shook her head and swallowed against what felt like a dirt clod stuck in her throat. "I figured Jed might have told you. We never had any. Actually, we tried several times, but they all ended in miscarriages, and the last one made it impossible."

His forehead creased and he reached for Paige's hand. "Oh, no. I'm so sorry. I wish Jed had told me. Then I wouldn't have mentioned it. I can see how sad it makes you."

She shook her head and bit into her bottom lip. "It's okay. It was a long time ago. I thought I had dealt with it, but now, I think because of Mom, it's all fresh again." She dug in her purse for a tissue. "I didn't tell you about Hazel either, the lady who was in your mom's room. I just recently made friends with her and she passed away last week. It hit me so hard." Tears rolled down her cheeks. "I still can't talk about it and I'm supposed to go to her funeral tomorrow."

Nicole slid their plates in front them and apologized for the lengthy wait.

Reed thanked her and asked for refills on their iced teas. He glanced over at Paige. "I hope I haven't ruined your meal. I'm so sorry."

The edges of her lips curled upward and she shook her head. "No, I'll find a way to stuff all this in." She eyed the platter, heaped with hot fries covered with salt, parsley, and garlic. "Let's find something cheerful to discuss while we eat."

Nicole topped off their teas and disappeared to help another customer.

Reed ate a handful of fries. "Oh, my gosh. These are so good." He reached for more. "I've got something. I saw the signs all over town for the Harvest Festival. I can't believe they're still doing them. I haven't been to one since I was a kid."

"Oh, yeah, it's even bigger than it was before. Much posher than just a simple fall festival. All the city folks flock out for it. Now, it's Apples, Ales, and Arts. There is every kind of apple confection you can imagine and tons of microbrews. Food trucks and vendors come from all over each year. I was here last year covering the store when Mom went on a trip with her friends. It was so busy."

"Maybe I can talk you into going with me?" He arranged the tomatoes and lettuce on his bun and smashed it on top of the thick burger. "We could grab Jed and force him to go, too."

She cut her burger in half. "I was toying with the idea of staying open on Sunday that weekend for the business but haven't decided."

"How about I volunteer to help you Saturday, then you close Sunday and give yourself the day off? Mom tells me you have a standing date with her to work on your artwork together on Sundays. You could do that and then we could spend the rest of the day enjoying the festival. I'll even volunteer to dress up and wave one of those big arrows to get people to shop on Saturday."

TAMMY L. GRACE

She laughed and snorted, almost choking on her first bite. "Hmm...I'm sure Mom has an old costume or two in the attic. What could I make you dress up as?" Her eyes went wide. "It would really be fun if I could say you're a best-selling author in disguise."

He held up his hands. "You are determined, aren't you? If it was up to me, I would tell you, but I've signed a legal document." He took another swallow from his glass. "I can tell it's going to be much more difficult to keep my secret here than in New York. Nobody knew me or cared. I could take my laptop to a coffeeshop and write for hours and it wouldn't raise an eyebrow. You're going to have to help me keep a low profile here. You're the only one who knows, and I don't want it to get out."

Her eyes widened. "Good thing Gladys can't talk. She's in tight with the editor at the newspaper and he's a buttinsky." She raised her hand. "I swear not to tell anyone, but I'm persistent, so I'll be doing my best to figure it out. If I guess, you have to promise to tell me."

He frowned and hesitated, picking up another handful of fries. "I know you, Paige, you'll just keep hounding me and guessing every name on the list. Like you used to pester me and Jed when we were writing notes to girls, always wanting to know who."

She laughed at the memory he stirred. She would listen outside Jed's bedroom door and try to hear what they were saying and had got caught more than once. "In the spirit of full transparency, I may have had the tiniest of crushes on you." She used her finger and thumb to show him just how tiny.

He threw his head back and chuckled. "Okay, as uncool as it was, I thought you were pretty cute, even though you were Jed's pain-in-the-butt little sister."

Her cheeks reddened and she reached for another fry to stuff in her mouth. She'd had no idea he'd even noticed her. At least not in that way.

She took hold of her iced tea glass and extended it to him. "Here's to youthful crushes."

He smiled and clinked her glass with his. "Cheers."

She was stuffed after eating all the fries and opted to take half the burger home. He grabbed the check from Nicole before Paige even noticed it and slipped his credit card into the mason jar they used to deliver it.

"My treat," he said with a smile.

"That's sweet of you. Totally unnecessary, but thank you."

After signing the credit card receipt, he helped her with her coat and held the door for her as they stepped onto the sidewalk. As they took slow steps together, she didn't want the evening to end. Visiting with him was like an escape from reality. His laugh and smile, not to mention his eyes, still had the ability to send a tingle of excitement through her. It took her right back to high school, when Reed would pass her in the hallway and catch her eye and say hello. "Feel like coming back to the house for a cup of tea?"

"Sounds great. Jed has a meeting at the store tonight and said he'd be late, so I've got nowhere to be."

The Winey Widows had left and locked the door, using the spare key her mom always kept in the cash register. When Paige unlocked the door, she bent and picked up the key, which she knew Norma had shoved through the mail slot. She had watched over the shop a few times for her mom and knew the drill. She put the key in the register before leading Jed through the door and into the kitchen.

Gladys was waiting on the other side of the door, her tail swishing in anticipation of company. None of the ladies were pet owners, so they would have paid Gladys little attention while Paige was gone.

When Reed followed Paige through the door, Gladys turned in circles before sitting and offering him a paw. "She is a character, isn't she?" He bent and took her paw.

"Mom was convinced she was a furry human, and the more I'm around her, the more I'm beginning to agree." She filled the electric kettle and went through the boxes of tea in the cupboard.

He walked around the kitchen, Gladys on his heels. "Wow, this is like stepping back in time. I had some of my best moments in this house."

She added hot water to their cups. "I've got funeral cookies and brownies in the freezer if you'd like some."

He wrinkled his nose. "I think I'll pass. I'm stuffed, and advertising them as funeral cookies sort of takes the fun out of them." He winked at her.

A giggle erupted and then she couldn't stop laughing. A snort escaped and then they were both laughing. She took a few deep breaths and swiped at the corners of her eyes. Happy tears this time. "I'm sorry. You're right about the idea of funeral cookies."

Stifling another laugh, he added, "Don't go into copywriting." He carried both cups into the large living area, where they each chose one of the leather recliners. Her mom hadn't upgraded her furniture in a long time, and when Paige had moved in, she brought the almost new furniture from her house in Albany, giving the room an updated look compared to her mom's old floral couches.

"You mentioned you have to attend Hazel's funeral tomorrow. I could go with you if you'd like?"

His kindness touched her heart. "That's so nice of you. You really would do that?"

"Sure. It's easier to face tough things when you have a friend with you. You say the time and I'll be there."

"It's at eleven o'clock at the church with a reception out at Aspen Grove. I'm just going to close the store for a couple of hours."

"I'll come by the store at a quarter to."

"Thank you. That really does make me feel better."

She settled into the chair and cradled the warm cup in her hands. You would think the bookstore that took up half of the downstairs would alleviate the necessity of bookcases, but her mother had a wall of them, filled with her favorites.

Reed looked toward the staircase. "I remember that

little alcove under the stairs, where your dad made those shelves and built-in couch for your mom."

She nodded. "It's still there. It was her favorite little spot to curl up and read. I loved it when I was a kid."

He took a sip from his cup. "I drove by Mom and Dad's old place today. It's just not the same. I was glad I had already left home when they moved from here. This was a perfect place to be a kid. I know your circumstances for coming home are terrible, but I'm glad you're able to come here. Come home."

Her throat tightened and she took a sip of the warm spiced tea. "Me, too."

CHAPTER 9

*P*aige couldn't bear the thought of wearing the same black dress she had worn to her Mom's funeral and opted for a black skirt and blouse instead.

Her stomach recoiled at the idea of food, so she settled on tea for breakfast and got an early start in the bookstore. Jed stopped by with Bentley, and they took Gladys with them to the hardware store. Now she wouldn't have to worry about her when she closed the store to attend Hazel's service.

With Reed's idea of Wishing Tree cards percolating, she ordered a supply of thick linen paper. She already had a powerful computer, scanner, printer, and all the software an illustrator needed. The investment in paper and time would be her only outlay, and since part of doing this project would be therapy, she wasn't worried about recouping her costs.

If she was happy with the cards, she'd add them to

bookstore and include them in the online store to see if she could sell more of them.

Once she had the designs perfected, she could print them out in mass.

As promised, Reed arrived in time for them to get to the church and say goodbye to Hazel. The pastor captured Hazel's essence and spirit, along with her strong faith, in his message of hope. At the end of the service, they stood in line to extend their condolences to her son, Robert.

As they inched forward, Paige recognized Hazel's smile in her son's.

When it was their turn, she introduced herself and Reed.

Robert clasped her hand in both of his. "I'm so glad to meet you, Paige." Tears filled his eyes. "Your visits and friendship meant the world to Mom. And to me. I'll never be able to thank you for that. The innkeeper told me the Wishing Tree had magical powers and urged me to tie a wish to it. I just did it to appease her, but then you and your sweet dog showed up and befriended my mom."

He shrugged and reached out to hug Paige. "Now, I'm a believer."

"I need to show you something," Paige said softy. Tears fell from her eyes as she fumbled in her purse and pulled out the card with the orange ribbon.

Robert's eyes went wide. "Oh, my gosh. You took my wish?"

She smiled. "Not exactly. My dog, Gladys, brought

it to me. It's a long story, but I'm so happy to have met your mom and so very sorry for your loss. She was a wonderful lady."

He thanked her again and they moved to let the next people in line greet him.

Paige let out a long breath as they walked outside.

Reed linked his arm through hers and took her hand, "Shall we head out for the reception and stop in and say hello to Mom?"

Through blurry eyes, she nodded, thankful for his strong shoulder and the warmth of his hand.

THE STORE WAS busy all week and Paige's renewed interest in her artwork made the days fly by. In preparation for the festival at the end of the month, Jed sent over a couple of guys from the hardware store to install white twinkly lights around the windows and in the shrubs and bushes surrounding the house. The town had already decorated the trees lining the sidewalk and throughout the town square. They'd soon be stringing larger globe lights across the entire square and getting it shipshape for the big event.

She and Gladys stopped in to say hello to Florence on her Thursday visit at Aspen Grove. They found her sitting on the edge of her bed, admiring her easel and the partially finished watercolor on it.

Florence had sketched the edge of one of the buildings and was making the bucket of deep purple chrysanthemums perched on the steps the focal point. She could only work on it in twenty-minute increments, since standing in one place wasn't easy. They'd visited for a few minutes over a cup of tea, and Paige told her how excited she was about dipping her toe back into her art with the greeting card idea Reed had suggested.

Just like with Hazel, the visit was enjoyable and moved too quickly. Soon Paige ushered Gladys out the door to hurry back to the house.

Now, each night for dinner, instead of it being her and Jed, Reed joined them.

Once they finished off the casseroles, Jed vowed to make pizza at Woody's a weekly habit and offered to cook something on the grill once a week. Reed was willing to bring takeout from any of the restaurants and handle the food shopping since he had the most free time.

Paige wasn't much of a cook but offered to dig through her mother's recipe box and find some favorite slow-cooker recipes, since the last thing she wanted to do when she closed the store was cook a meal.

She found that each day was getting a bit easier and credited having Reed around with her improved outlook. The house was filled with conversation and laughter again, and although it wasn't the same as having her mom, the three of them were making new memories and finding happiness in moments.

Over dinner on Friday, takeout from the Crooked

Porch, the two men convinced Paige she ought to move into the master bedroom with the larger bathroom. She had her computer and printer set up in the guest bedroom, and it didn't offer much room. The master was big enough to accommodate a desk and her supplies and had the best view of the square and the Wishing Tree for inspiration.

Paige resisted at first, thinking it was disrespectful, but, after a few hours of listening to the two of them, understood the practicality of it. She hated the thought of discarding any of her mom's things but, at the same time, knew it didn't make sense to leave her clothes hanging in her closet. She'd go through them and ask the ladies to take anything they might wear when they came over on Monday.

Jed and Reed both offered to help her, but she wanted to do it alone. She was sure to be a blubbering mess and didn't need an audience.

With that in mind, she opted to skip Jed's offer of meeting up for pizza Saturday night, and instead, she and Gladys stood staring at her mom's closet.

Some of the clothes held no memories, but others, like the soft cashmere cardigan her mother had loved, made the breath catch in Paige's throat. Her mom had worn it often and it held the scent of her perfume.

Paige slipped it over her shirt, hoping it would give her the strength she needed to finish the job.

The closet was large, with rods on both sides, top and bottom, along with space for coats and dresses, and shelves for sweaters and shoes. She noticed one side still held a few of her dad's flannel shirts. She buried her nose in one of them, not sure if she imagined the scent of sawdust that had seemed to follow him everywhere or if it could still be in the fibers of his shirts.

There was more than enough room to keep anything Paige wanted, so she started separating items, segregating everything that could be given away and moving items she wanted to keep to the area next to her dad's shirts.

Anything that triggered a strong memory or made her teary-eyed, she moved to the area she was keeping.

Margot hadn't been an extravagant dresser, not like Agnes and Jean, who had outfits that looked like they came from pages of fashion magazines. Cecilia had eclectic taste and Norma tended to favor plain clothes. Margot had been in the middle, choosing timeless and classy pieces that could be mixed and matched. She and Paige were similar in size, so anything Paige liked, she could use rather than just keep in the closet.

She finished and surveyed her progress, deciding whatever the ladies didn't take, she'd ask them to donate to the local charity shop. Next, she tackled the dresser drawers and added to the basket of things that could be given away, consolidating what she was keeping into one large drawer.

Paige wanted to keep all of her mom's jewelry, which wasn't much and was kept in a pretty wooden box atop her dresser.

Next, Gladys followed her to her childhood

bedroom, where she made a few trips to transfer her own clothes into the master closet. Jed and Reed would have to move the computer desk for her tomorrow.

In the bathroom, the subtle vanilla scent of her mom's favorite shower gel lingered, and she shut her eyes to inhale it. She hoped the scent never left. It was comforting, like her mother had been.

Her dad's side of the vanity was bare, with all the drawers available. Paige deposited her own toiletries in those drawers and left her mother's where they were. She'd tackle that another day. She was too exhausted to consider throwing away her mom's toothbrush or see the silver strands in her hairbrush. She wasn't ready to discard all those little things that her mother had touched and used every day.

Her mom had been so strong after her dad passed away. Paige had never given her enough credit, never truly understood her pain. Until now.

She glanced over and looked at Gladys, who was sitting, watching as she finished organizing the drawers. "I think you deserve some of your favorite cheese cookies, and I'm going to have a big bowl of ice cream as a reward."

She turned out the light as they left and couldn't help but smile at the warm glow of lights from the Wishing Tree that filled the room.

Surprised at how well she had slept in her mom's bed, Paige woke later than usual on Sunday. She showered in the oversize walk-in shower and used her mom's shower gel, delighted to have found three new bottles in the linen closet last night. She'd savor them and made a mental note to buy more before they discontinued it.

Although not much of a cook, Paige did enjoy baking and was craving some of her mom's pumpkin bread. Carefully following her mom's instructions on the recipe card to the last detail, she put together a double batch and slipped the pans into the oven.

She browsed the recipe box again and found her mom's recipe for chili and put it together. She could make some cornbread, too, and was sure Jed and Reed would enjoy it, since it had been a staple at their house when they'd been growing up.

As the pumpkin bread baked, filling the house with the aroma that always made her think of fall and her mom's kitchen, she did a few household chores. While the bread cooled, she and Gladys curled into the alcove under the stairs, where her mother had spent many a happy afternoon, and selected a book from the shelf.

As she scanned all the books, she wondered if Reed could be the author of any of them.

She took a book and examined the jacket and the author photo. It was an author she'd read and had seen interviewed on television, so she knew it wasn't Reed. He had said the publisher liked the intrigue of people not knowing who the author was, so it stood to reason there would be no author photo on the cover jacket. That could narrow her search. Unless they had used a model or stock photo for an author image.

She read a few chapters, with Gladys snuggled next to her, snoring softly. She could have spent the whole day there but knew how important it was to the people who were expecting Gladys, not to mention Mrs. Walker, so she crawled from under the throw blanket and loaded up her supplies, a thick chunk of still warm pumpkin bread, and Gladys.

They turned out of the driveway and headed for Aspen Grove.

Once there, it only took a few minutes of watching Gladys interact and delight the residents gathered in the large common room for Paige's spirits to lift. Her mom had been so wise to spend her time volunteering here. Being around all these people, who lived a very small life, made her realize how lucky she was and how much helping others helped her. Instead of sinking into her own grief, Margot had chosen to be of service to others and to her community. It made Paige want to be a better person.

Soon, they wandered over to the other building and found Florence waiting for them. Her eyes lit up at the pumpkin bread and she groaned when she took a bite. "This is so yummy. Thanks for bringing me a treat."

While she snacked, Paige checked out her easel, noting her progress, with the flowers fully detailed now and the painting almost finished. "It looks like you did quite a bit of work in the last few days. I like it."

Florence nodded. "It's not a masterpiece but sure helps pass the time. Faith said I should teach a class in the other building. They're always looking for ideas and several people have inquired about watercolors."

"Oh, that would be great. You're such a wonderful teacher and I bet you'd enjoy it."

Florence's eyes sparkled as she nodded. "I think it sounds great. I've actually been giving some thought to moving in there, when I'm up to it. Reed and I were talking yesterday, and as much as I hate the idea, it makes the most sense. Faith said she'd give me a full tour when I'm able to walk a bit farther."

"It's actually very nice. I was surprised, but it's more like an apartment building in a way. Everyone seems very happy. You should definitely take Faith up on a tour."

She nodded and stroked Gladys's ears. "Show me your sketches. I've been dying to see them."

Paige took them out of her bag and placed them on the bed.

Florence smiled. "Oh, they are all gorgeous, Paige. I love the seasons."

"That was Reed's idea. Well, inspired by the old drawings I did that hang in Mom's shop." She pointed at the winter one, with the branches covered in snow. "I'm toying with stringing some colored lights in this one, just to give it a pop. The others all have more color, but this one is sort of blah."

"Oh, yes, I think that's a good idea or you could just add a pretty red ribbon on the trunk."

"Ooh, I like that idea. I'll try it both ways. She took one of the copies she had made and added a ribbon while Gladys stretched next to Florence for a belly rub. Paige put a string of lights on the lower section of the tree and then used her colored pencils before turning it to show Florence. "Which to do you like best?"

"Oh, that's a tough one. I like them both. You should do some of each. You're not limited to just one idea, you know." She winked at Paige and studied all the drawings for a few minutes. "In fact, you could add little touches to each of them to make some of them different, ribbons, flags for the Fourth of July, or little touches of flowers here and there, depending on the season. It could be fun to have a variety."

Paige realized she had a tendency to look at things in a black-and-white fashion sometimes, especially this last year. Florence was right, she didn't have to just choose one design for each season, she could do whatever she wanted. She was only limited by her imagination. She'd forgotten that lately. Loss and trauma could do that to you.

While they continued their visit, Florence indulged in another piece of pumpkin bread and a fresh cup of tea. Paige made notes on the copies of her drawings with ideas for each season while they chatted.

Florence nibbled on the last bite of her pumpkin bread and smiled. "Jed is so kind to offer Reed a place to stay. It means so much to me to have him here and to know he is enjoying himself is even better. It reminds me of when they were young boys, always hanging out with each other and having fun."

Paige nodded and finished her tea. "I think it's great for Jed to have Reed around. I think he spends far too much time alone, so having a roommate is great, especially a good friend."

When she realized it was getting dark outside, she stood. "Oh, I better get going. I put chili in the slow cooker for Jed and Reed. I need to make some cornbread to go with it."

"That sounds lovely, dear. I'm so thankful Reed has reconnected with you, and Jed, of course. I've never seen him so lighthearted. I can tell he's delighted to be back in Linden Falls and I think you might be a big reason for that."

CHAPTER 10

Friday night, Jed had to work late to get the store ready for the busy weekend, so Reed brought dinner, and he and Paige enjoyed rich and buttery lobster mac and cheese and a pear salad from the Crooked Porch. In between sales, Paige had put her brand-new greeting cards in plastic sleeves and added them to the card rack, giving them prominent placement near the counter, where people waiting in line might see them. She also bundled together a few sets and tied them with pretty orange ribbons.

The town was bustling with activity, with many people having already arrived for the festival that would kick off in the morning.

Reed said he'd spent most of his day writing but had worked in a quick visit with his mom.

He carried his empty plate to the sink. "Mom seems much more open to moving into Aspen Grove. She said she mentioned it to you."

"Yeah, I was surprised, but I think she's realized she can't stay on her own. Oh, and Faith is so bubbly and charismatic, I'm sure she encouraged your mom. I told her I was surprised at how nice it was."

"Faith gave me a tour, and I thought so, too. Not at all what I thought it would be and so much brighter and more open than where Mom is now." He collected her dishes and went about rinsing them. "They're also free to leave, if they still drive, or spend holidays with their families. Faith had to remind me it's not a prison, it's just a safe environment for people who need a little extra care."

Paige nodded. "Mom always raved about it, and honestly when she said she wouldn't mind living there when the time came, I didn't think much of it. Now, after spending time there, I know I would have felt comfortable leaving her there. It really feels like a big family instead of an institution."

He filled the kettle and took out two mugs. "I called Lynn and told her about it, and she agreed it sounds like the best plan. So, I think we're going to sell Mom's place and then use the money to pay for her stay out there. It's not cheap, but I think it's the right decision."

Paige took her mug and led the way into the living room, with Gladys following. She sat on the end of the couch next to the side table. "What's nice and unique about Aspen Grove is that, if something happens, she can stay right there and get all the care she needs. That would give me peace of mind knowing she wouldn't have to be completely uprooted if she became ill or needed a bit of extra care. I think it's less traumatic for the patients and why it seems more like a home than a hospital."

He smiled at her. "It's nice to have someone to talk to about all this. Lynn is so far away, and with her family, she just doesn't have the bandwidth to do much beyond telling me to do what I think is best. My dad's death was like your mom's. Quick and unexpected, so there were no decisions to be made."

She nodded. "I remember I used to hear about people dying in their sleep and was always so sad for their families. They never got the chance to say goodbye or even get used to the idea of them being gone. Now, having had Dad go more slowly, then Danny suffering through all he did, and Mom going in her sleep, all I can say is they're both equally awful. I console myself when I think about Mom and know that she didn't have to suffer or go through horrible medical procedures and just slipped away peacefully, I hope. It's harder for me, right now, because I had no warning, but watching Danny slowly deteriorate and then give up was worse for me. I was exhausted and I know he was. It was months of despair with very few hopeful moments, and I wouldn't wish it on my worst enemy."

"Being a kid was so much easier than being an adult." He reached for the box of tissues and set it next to her.

She shook her head. "Sorry, I still can't talk about either of them without crying."

"I don't blame you. I can't even think about losing my mom. When I got the call that she broke her hip, my heart just sank. It seems like that is the beginning of the end for so many people her age. I just want her to live as long as she can and for her to be healthy and happy. I don't want her warehoused in some horrible place where nobody interacts with her and she's just lying there waiting to go."

"And I don't want that to happen to me, either. With Mom gone, I've really been worried, thinking about my own mortality. I have no kids. Jed's kids are my only younger family members. It's weird to say it aloud, but I feel like the guardrail is gone and I'm on the edge. The next one to go, you know? I know it sounds awful and I never thought about it until now."

"I think that's natural and wouldn't hit you until they're gone." His voice cracked and he took a sip from his cup. "Like I said, I can't even think about it. Losing Dad was hard on us and I wasn't ready. I hadn't asked him all the questions I needed to and still miss his sage advice." He shut his eyes, and Paige reached across the cushion to take his hand and gave it a firm squeeze.

He tightened his fingers around hers. "He was so calm and practical. Mom is sort of the opposite. She's not one to think things through and analyze them. That was always Dad's thing. I miss it and him. Like now, he would know what to do, and I've been trying to approach this situation with Mom like I think he would." Gladys moved from her spot and leaned against his legs, getting as close to him as possible without climbing into his lap.

Paige smiled. "That's because your mom is so creative, and we tend to be poor planners. Your dad would be so proud of you. I think you're doing the right thing by encouraging your mom to move into Aspen Grove."

He nodded. "That makes me feel better. It's hard to know what to do. I liked it better when my parents were in charge."

"You don't realize how carefree our lives were until you grow up and have to deal with everything. I think that's part of what I'm feeling with Mom gone. It's not like I'm an orphan. I have Jed, but that security that comes from knowing I could reach out to Mom is gone. She was the one I turned to most this last year."

He moved closer to her and slipped his arm around her shoulders. "Now, you've got me, too."

She dabbed at her eyes while Gladys repositioned herself between them. "How about we find something to watch?" She picked up the remote and began flicking through options. They settled on the new season of *Doc Martin*, discovering they were both fans of the quirky show set in Cornwall.

The gorgeous scenery and the eccentric characters soon had them laughing and putting aside their heavy conversation. After the first episode, he refilled their mugs, and she reached for her mom's heavy throw blanket and threw it over her lap, stretching it out to give Reed enough for his legs, too.

They laughed when Gladys took the opportunity to come up through the bottom and fill the space between them, her snout on Paige's lap.

Hours later, Paige woke, her arm asleep with Reed's head resting against it.

Gladys was no longer there, but with a quick peek, she saw the dog had found the end of the couch more comfortable.

Paige wiggled her fingers, trying to get the needles of numbness out of them.

She sat there for a few more minutes, unsure what to do. She hated to disturb him but had to get up.

Quietly and carefully, she slid out from under him and added a couple of throw pillows to the corner so he'd have something under his head.

He squirmed a bit and then settled into the new space.

She added another blanket over the top of him and put her finger to her lips when Gladys met her eyes. It was three o'clock in the morning and way too late for him to go back to Jed's.

She turned off the television and tiptoed to the staircase. Gladys elected to stay behind and nestled close to the edge of the couch. Paige smiled at her, thinking what a good girl she was to stay with him.

He had talked through a lot of feelings, and he needed the comfort tonight more than she did.

AFTER A COUPLE more hours of sleep, Paige woke and got ready for the day. When she came downstairs, she found the throw blankets folded but no Reed and no Gladys. She took a look outside and saw his car was still parked on the side of the house. She also noticed that the vendors and food trucks were already staking out prime spots in the square.

Paige only hoped Calvin from the newspaper hadn't walked by in the middle of the night or early this morning and noticed Reed's car.

That would get tongues wagging.

She hurried back inside and got to work in the bookstore.

Last week, Reed had suggested he set up a small area outside near the sidewalk and have a few things on display to entice shoppers or capture their interest for spontaneous purchases. Jed had already had his guys drop off folding tables and chairs to fashion a makeshift sales area.

She was gathering the boxes of product to display when the bells chimed on the front door, and she looked up to see Reed's smiling face. He was carrying a box from the bakery along with a drink tray from Doc's Fountain. Gladys was prancing behind him, looking pleased with herself.

"We went for a quick walk, and I stopped by the hardware store to apologize to Jed for not coming home last night."

Her eyes widened. "What did my brother have to say about your revelation?"

He wiggled his eyebrows and handed her a cup of her favorite chai tea latte, sprinkled with cinnamon. "He gave me a good ribbing but was convinced I was a perfect gentleman."

She noticed the sprinkling of sugar granules along his lips.

"It looks like you might have sampled an apple cider donut." She grinned and opened the box to take one for herself and found a small bag of pumpkin dog treats nestled among the sugar-crusted donuts.

He licked his lips and laughed. "Caught me. They are so good. I'd forgotten how much I've missed this place." He swooped in and kissed her cheek. "And not just because of the donuts."

Before she could respond or even try to hide her blushing, he hurried to the door. "I've got to go grab a shower, but I'll be back in a few minutes."

She giggled and looked down at Gladys. "He's a fun guy, isn't he?"

Gladys thumped her tail against the floor and kept her eye on the donut, watching as Paige took her first bite. She shook her head at the dog. "These aren't good for you, but you obviously have charmed Reed." She dug out one of the cookies and Gladys crunched on it, winking at her.

In between bites, Paige gathered up the fabric she found in her mom's supply closet and got the tables covered. She made sure her basket of cards was prominent in addition to several of the popular gift items like scarves, mugs, and candles.

Reed returned in time to eat two more donuts and arrange a few new releases on bookstands while she went back inside to get the cash box and the credit card gizmo that could be used on her cell phone.

Visitors were already roaming the sidewalks and pouring into Doc's and the bakery down the street. She showed Reed how to swipe a credit card using the device, and they processed a mock sale to test it. They traded cell phones so he could call her if he needed something and he urged Gladys to stay with him, telling her she was a good chick magnet who could lure shoppers to him.

Paige chuckled and headed indoors.

Within a few minutes, the shop was filled with tourists. They browsed and chatted and thankfully bought tons of books and other items. In addition to the delicious smell of donuts in the air, each time the door opened, it brought in the scent of kettle corn and apple pie.

By midmorning, the festival was in full swing, with thousands of visitors descending upon the tiny village.

While Paige appreciated the business, she was glad she had decided to close the next day. By early afternoon, she'd had her fill of the hurried city dwellers and their obsession with their phones, along with the young mothers who were miffed that she didn't allow strollers inside the store. Mind you, strollers were now all-terrain vehicles, wider than the aisles and outfitted with racks and storage compartments. Her mom had made the decision years ago, and she put up her hand-lettered sign, reminding customers of the rule and the small size of the store.

Sunday was usually quieter, with most of the visitors making a day trip out of the festival or, if they decided to stay overnight, finding a place with more lodging options. It didn't take much to fill the Wishing Tree Inn and the other smaller bed-and-breakfasts that dotted the countryside.

By noon, most of the vendors had started packing up to head home.

Pasting a friendly smile on her face, Paige handed a bag to the last of the group of women, outfitted in their five-hundred-dollar yoga pants and hoodie ensembles with designer cross-body bags, most of whom, she guessed, had never used their clothes for working out. They had asked where they could find a juicery.

Paige pointed them in the direction of Doc's Fountain, knowing they did a few juice drinks and smoothies.

She noticed Jed out front at Reed's table, and a few minutes later, he came through the door with a cardboard container. "Hey, I picked you and Reed up one of those gourmet grilled cheese sandwiches I remember you liked from the food truck."

"Wow, thanks. I was just thinking about lunch, and looking at the crowd, I figured I'd be stuck foraging for something here. How'd you get through?"

He grinned. "Turns out the guy forgot his extra extension cords and I loaned him a couple." He tilted his head in the direction of the front door. "Go on and sit down and eat with Reed. I can watch the store for a few minutes." He grabbed a handful of the red bags hanging on a hook behind the counter. "He said he needs more bags."

He hooked them on her finger and she went out the door.

Along with the cheesy goodness and bacon brushed with maple syrup on perfectly toasted bread, Jed had also delivered a cup of sparkling apple cider, a favorite of hers.

While they ate, they waited on a few more customers. She tapped on her phone a few times and, with wide eyes, turned it toward Reed so he could see their impressive total for the day.

"Wow, that seems like a healthy sales number to me." He raised his brows.

She nodded. "That's an epic sales day. We've had a great month, but this is the best day yet, and it's not over."

She eyed the basket and noticed only a few of her greeting cards remained.

Gladys loved cheese, and Paige couldn't resist giving her a generous chunk of melted cheddar. He finished his last bite. "That was, hands down, the best grilled cheese ever. Why don't you stay open tomorrow morning, just to catch as much business as you can? We can stop by and say hello to Mom tonight and let her know. She'll understand if you beg off tomorrow."

She wrinkled her nose. "I was just thinking how happy I'd be not to have to pretend to care about the city slickers. I've forgotten how demanding they can be. Most of the leaf peepers we get are sweet older ladies on a group tour who have traveled to get here and are usually a delight. This younger generation gets on my nerves."

He laughed and said, "Maybe you need a sign that says 'Get off my lawn.' You sound a bit like a curmudgeon."

"I'll think about it." With a sarcastic grin, she gathered the empty containers and took the rest of her sparkling cider inside.

Jed was finishing up a sale when she slipped in behind him. When the customer left, he pointed out the window. "I'll take Gladys back to the store with me. Bentley is bored and not getting much attention. I'll make sure they stay in my office so they don't wander off."

Paige thanked him. "Oh, and I decided to stay open a half day tomorrow. We're going to run and see Florence as soon as we close up tonight. Do you want to meet up afterward for pizza, my treat?"

"Sure, I'll call Woody and get us a table now." Woody didn't take reservations, but he always took care of his regular customers, and Jed was one of his best.

The hours passed by with more customers and sales, and when she put the last of her greeting cards in a bag, she thought of her mom. She would have been so happy to see her enjoying drawing again and making a little money from her talent. She'd have to print out some more tonight. Maybe she could talk Reed into helping her get them ready for tomorrow.

Despite loving the festival, she had been dreading this weekend, the first one without her mom. Paige was worried it would be too overwhelming. Having Reed around helped. His presence made it easier.

Instead of the sad day she'd feared, he had made sure it was fun and his ideas were good ones. Watching Reed chat with the customers and recommend hand-made soaps and pretty scarves to the women made her smile.

Reed was a good guy.

Even better than she remembered.

CHAPTER 11

*a*fter a busy Sunday morning, and a rush of customers each time they started to take down the displays and close, they ended up staying open until three o'clock. By then, most of the tourists had packed up their cars and headed home.

The locals, including Jed and his staff, who were tasked with much of the takedown duties, hung around for the end-of-the-festival celebratory dinner.

After all the vendors cleared out, everyone gathered for corn chowder, lamb stew, and apple pie. The lights strung above the square made for a beautiful setting, and Reed found a spot at a table under the Wishing Tree.

Jed sat with his staff, who had worked extra hard all weekend, and they were all celebrating a job well done.

Atop the tables, covered in deep purple and bronze fabric, candles flickered from a variety of glass holders and jars people had contributed. Despite the rustic nature of their simple dinner on the square, Paige thought it was gorgeous. It was a perfect, crisp fall evening, and the warm chowder and fresh bread hit the spot.

A local band entertained everyone with songs and showcased a talented fiddler. Several couples took to dancing, and the crowd clapped along, in tune with the music. As they listened, Reed reached for her hand and held it, rubbing his thumb over her knuckles.

A gale of laughter erupted, and Paige looked for the source and saw their newest Linden Falls resident, Verity Joseph, in Jack Darby's arms as he swung her around, then tipped her back to bring about her delight. Her happiness was palpable and made Paige smile. She made a mental reminder to reach out to Verity and ask her for coffee. She needed to make some friends her own age. Maybe she'd invite Janie from the inn, too. Start their own little club to rival the Winey Widows, or at least make them think they had some competition.

The Wishing Tree behind them caught her gaze. Neva had been in her glory this weekend, passing out cards with ribbons to anyone who wanted to tie a wish onto the tree, and it was brimming with them. Most of the leaves had fallen and the wishes had taken their places on the bare branches.

Paige looked up at the cards fluttering in the slight breeze. Her mother would have loved the day, and she wished she could have been there. As she looked beyond the branches to the sky, she saw a bright star shoot across the dark expanse. The sight gave her a shiver. Maybe her mom was there. She liked to think of her watching over Linden Falls.

The evening was a bit surreal. Paige never would have imagined sitting here, under her mom's tree, just over a month after losing her, and feeling a spark of happiness, like maybe she'd survive after all.

She glanced at Reed and met his eyes.

He smiled and she knew he was responsible for the new glimmer of hope in her heart. The hope for the future she hadn't been sure she'd ever feel again.

After everyone had cleared the square and all the litter was bagged and ready to be disposed of, Paige and Reed took their pie to go.

They strolled down the street, where they grabbed a couple of hot chocolates before Doc's closed.

Then they wandered back to the house, admiring the twinkling lights in all the storefronts along the way, including those gracing the windows and shrubs in front of the bookstore. There was something so inviting about them.

"Wait just a minute before we go in," Paige said, coming to a stop before the door.

She stood still for a moment and marveled at the refuge her mother had created. It wasn't just a store, it was a haven for the community. Paige was happy Norma had volunteered to start up the knitting group. She pictured them sitting around the fire on snowy days, sipping tea, working their needles, and most of all telling stories.

She unlocked the door and Reed followed her inside and into the kitchen. Gladys was passed out and barely opened her eye to look at them before closing it and snuggling back into her bed.

"What a weekend, huh?" Reed unwrapped his slice of pie.

"I'll say. I can't believe we sold out of cards again. That was a fabulous idea you had."

He grinned. "Don't sound so surprised. I have been known to have some pretty good ones over the years."

She laughed as she dug her fork into the flaky crust. "I didn't mean it like that. I'm just surprised they sold so well. I'm going to have to order some more paper and envelopes."

He sighed and met her eyes. "It was one of the best weekends I've had in months. I haven't been this happy, this relaxed in a long time. I'm always working, holed up in my apartment, ordering takeout, cranking out a book while getting an email asking me about the time-line for the next book. It's been wonderful to escape all of that."

She nodded. "I wasn't expecting to enjoy this week-end, but it's been fun. I'm glad you were here to share it with me."

He reached across the table and took her hand in his. "I love writing and what I do, but these last weeks, being here, it's made me wish I would have never left Linden Falls. When I was a kid, I couldn't wait to leave, but now, it seems like the best place in the world."

His words were too perfect for her to respond. She

didn't know what she was supposed to say, and she sure didn't want to ruin the moment.

Reed let her hand go and hers felt bereft without his.

He took a long sip from his cup. "I'm going to go into the city tomorrow. I'll be gone for a couple of days, so if you don't mind, could you check on Mom for me?"

She nodded. "Sure, no problem. Is everything okay? That's a long drive."

He rolled his eyes. "Four hours and I'm not looking forward to it, but it comes with the territory. I just have a meeting with my editor and another one with the marketing team. I'll be back Wednesday. I'll treat you to dinner. How about that little French place, Bistro Claudine?"

Her brows arched. "Ooh, fancy. I haven't been there, but the chef has been in the store a few times. I've heard great things about the food."

His eyes danced with excitement. "It's a date. I'll pick you up at seven."

They finished off the pie and tossed their empty cups in the trash. "I need to get going. I've got an early start in the morning."

She walked with him, out the back door and through the gate to the side yard, where he had parked. "Thanks again for all your help this weekend. I couldn't have done it without you."

She caught his grin in the dim light of the streetlamp.

"I'm sure you could have handled it. You're quite capable, Paige Duncan."

"Well, you made it much more fun."

He bent his head closer to hers and pressed his lips to hers. Despite the bittersweet memories of her husband, she welcomed the touch, the connection.

It shocked her, but she shut her eyes, breathing in that cedar scent she loved. She grabbed his shoulders, letting the kiss deepen.

Reed pulled away and shook his head, like he had water in his ear. "I'm sorry, I couldn't help myself. I've wanted to do that since we were kids." Underneath his laugh she heard the nervousness.

Embarrassment and excitement coursed through her. "I'm glad you did." She reached her head higher and kissed him again.

⤛⟫⟫

ON MONDAY after she closed the store and left it in the hands of the Winey Widows, she took one of the vases filled with fall flowers leftover from the festival, loaded Gladys into her SUV, and drove out to Aspen Grove. The dinner period was over and she found Florence in her pajamas, tucked into bed, reading. She got a glimpse at the title, but it was another she knew wasn't written by Reed.

Florence looked up from her book and smiled. "Oh, what a wonderful surprise. It's Monday, right?"

Paige set the flowers on her bedside table. "It is, but

since I skipped yesterday, I thought we'd pop out and check on you."

Florence narrowed her eyes. "Reed asked you to check on me, I bet."

"He did, but that's not the only reason." She moved the chair and took a seat, letting Gladys get up on the bed. "I wanted to tell you what a hit my illustrated cards were. We sold out, even after making more on Saturday night." She couldn't help a proud smile from creeping up.

Florence was thrilled for her. "Oh, that's terrific. They are stunning. I was thinking about them this weekend and thought you could get fancy and sprinkle some of them with glitter for the holidays."

"That would be pretty. A bit more time-consuming, but I could try a few sets and see how they sell."

"Reed called me from the road this morning and went on and on about what a great time he had this weekend. I'm so glad he's found you again. He's stressed thinking about getting my place ready to sell and figuring out what to do with all the stuff in the house. That's the part that makes me sad. I won't be able to bring much with me when I move into the other building." She shrugged. "It's not like I need any of it, and I know this is my decision, but it feels so final." Tears dotted her cheeks.

Paige patted her favorite teacher's arm. "I'm sorry. I know that can't be easy, and I understand how hard it is to accept a big change in your life."

Florence blotted the tissue against her eyes. "I know

you do, dear. I'm just having a little pity party. Reed is such a good son. He told me if I didn't want to sell the house, he'd pay for me to stay here as long as I needed."

Paige didn't believe it was possible to think more of Reed, but listening to his mom, her heart filled with affection for the man he had become.

Florence shook her head. "I, of course, told him that was ridiculous. There's no sense letting the old place sit there and deteriorate. His dad would roll over in his grave if I even considered such an impractical notion. I think it will just take me some time to come to accept it."

"You'll just have to downsize, but it's a small apartment, much bigger than this room. Faith showed me one and I saw a good-sized bedroom, with plenty of space for dressers and bookcases, a large living room, and a small kitchenette. You won't be doing any cooking, but you can store snacks. It's set up with a microwave and refrigerator, toaster, all that kind of stuff. I'm sure you can fit in your couch and a couple of chairs, a television, and a bookcase or side tables in the living space."

"Well, that sounds encouraging, dear," Florence said.

Paige nodded. "I'll make sure Faith gets you a floorplan and then you can draw in what you want to keep and how to fashion a little area for your art studio."

Her cloudy eyes brightened at the idea. "That would be wonderful. You're such a thoughtful young woman."

"I think they have some two-bedroom units, too, if

you find you need more room. Remember, Jed can order or make anything you need."

She rested her head against her pillows. "I'm not sure it has anything to do with space, dear. I think it's more wrapping my head around the fact that I'm no longer independent. No longer the person I thought I'd always be. I honestly don't feel old inside. I'm still the same person who chased after Reed and Lynn and all my students at school. It's only when I look in the mirror or go to do something that requires strength, or using my right leg, that I realize I'm old."

"Once your hip heals, you'll be back on your feet. And you can still pursue your art, Florence. Don't forget that."

Florence reached for another tissue. "I know. It's just…well, the last thing I want to do is be a burden to Reed or have Lynn worrying about me. I know it makes sense for me to stay here, and there's nothing wrong with it, it's just a big blow to my ego, I suppose."

"I know. I wish I could make you feel better," Paige said, feeling helpless.

Florence sighed and shut her eyes. "I'll be fine, I promise."

Paige reached for Gladys's leash and the dog hopped off the bed. "I know you will. Sleep well and we'll see you Thursday."

Florence was already asleep, and Paige guided Gladys to the door, where they slipped out without a sound.

CHAPTER 12

Wednesday, Paige's supply order arrived. She was happy to unpack them, as she was anxious to get started on making more cards and incorporating Florence's idea for some holiday varieties.

In between customers, she sketched a few variations of the winter tree, adding the storefronts in the distance, decorated for Christmas. She did another one with a snowman to the side of the tree and could picture it with touches of glitter.

Just after lunch, Gladys returned from her morning outing and sprawled out in front of the fire. While Paige nibbled on leftovers, she finished her monthly sales reports and put together what she hoped was her final holiday order for inventory.

With the leaves all but gone and the festival over, it was a slow sales day, and she was able to call Norma and give her the go-ahead on getting the knitters organized.

Then she did a quick scan of the giftware, making sure there was nothing else she needed to add to her order. Next, she looked at the small used books section, housed in a bookcase along the far wall. It always looked a bit messy and she had been trying to convince her mom to get rid of it.

Margot had liked the idea of providing inexpensive books to those who couldn't afford them and often didn't even charge the dollar or quarter price she advertised.

Paige went about trying to straighten and organize the shelves since they had become disheveled with all the weekend customers pawing through them.

Maybe she could get Jed to design one of those cute little free libraries she had seen online. That would accomplish what her mom wanted to do, letting people take a book if they wanted one and encouraging other people to donate their used books. That would free up more space inside for giftware or items like her cards.

Jed would have to figure out how to make the free library weatherproof so the books wouldn't get damaged in the wet winters Linden Falls sometimes had.

Once she had the shelves organized and a short list of a few more items to add to her order, it was time to close. She locked the door and rustled Gladys from her spot and into the house, then poured kibble into her bowl.

"You. Eat."

She left her to it and hurried upstairs to take stock of her wardrobe.

She hadn't been to an upscale restaurant in a long time. Perhaps the last time was when she and Danny had celebrated their anniversary at their favorite steakhouse last year. That had been in June, and she remembered she had worn the sleeveless purple wrap dress that she thought made her arms look fat, but Danny had assured her she looked beautiful. It had been a fabulous meal and a perfect night where they strolled through Capitol Park.

The bittersweet memory was another stark reminder of how life could change in a heartbeat. She would have never guessed that six months later, her husband's car would plunge into the icy river and he would be fighting for his life. Watching him endure so much for all those months and then seeing him lose hope and quit fighting had broken her.

Paige wasn't sure she would ever recover, but coming back here, back home, had been what she needed.

She decided to focus on the present.

With her working from home for most of her career, she had never invested in many clothes, preferring jeans and T-shirts or sweaters. After trying on several things, she finally decided on a nice pair of black pants, a matching turtleneck, and her mom's pretty merlot-colored wrap.

She opened her mom's jewelry box and added a

long Y necklace made with silver and beads that she had always admired and thought looked classy.

Gladys had joined her after she'd eaten, and now she lay curled on the floor, watching as Paige adjusted the necklace, the silver perfect against the black backdrop. She hunted for earrings that would work with it and found a pair she remembered her mom wearing with the necklace several times. They were silver with beaded drops that weren't an exact match, but close enough.

Paige didn't wear much makeup but took extra care tonight and applied mascara to her thick lashes, worked blush into her cheeks, and swiped a pretty lipstick that matched her wrap across her lips.

When she stood back and gazed into the mirror, she had to admit she looked nice.

Maybe she needed to wear makeup more often.

She went to the closet and slipped into a pair of low-heeled burgundy ankle boots her mom had given her for Christmas and put her hands on her hips.

"What do you think, Gladys?" The dog raised her head, yawned, and lay back down.

"Hmm, that stunning, huh?"

Paige looked out on the square, the lights from the Wishing Tree catching her eye. Her mom was right, it was a gorgeous view from up here, with all the trees along the walkways decorated with lights and her special tree in the center of the square, the sentinel, keeping watch over the entire town.

She turned out the light and headed downstairs.

When she reached the landing, the tinkle of Gladys's tags and the click of her nails on the wooden floor made Paige stop and wait for her. She had never understood her mother's attachment to the fluffy girl, but now, she couldn't imagine her life without her. She was such a comfort and always there to greet her and make her smile.

Now she understood why her mother had such an affection for her and credited the sweet dog with helping her get through sad days.

Having the dog's presence in the big, old house made Paige feel not so alone. Now, instead of complaining about cleaning the floors each day to collect her golden fur, she was happy to have that chore, since it meant her best friend was there to keep her company and snuggle with her each evening.

That was when she missed her mom the most. When the house was quiet and there was nothing to occupy her mind, nothing except memories.

Paige couldn't have pictured herself sleeping with a seventy-pound golden retriever, but now she thought it tantamount to abuse to make Gladys sleep on the floor. Sometimes, when Paige was thinking too much or feeling especially vulnerable, Gladys would seek her out and place her chin on her leg or in her hand. When Paige would look into her gentle eyes, she could swear her mom was there, assuring her she would be okay and things would get better.

Paige glanced at the clock in the kitchen.

Reed would be arriving in a few minutes. She

reached in the fridge and pulled out a few chunks of leftover chicken and fed them to Gladys as a guilty treat for having to leave her. She petted the top of her head as she happily chewed them. "You're the best friend a girl could have. Don't be mad because I have a date."

In mid-chew, Gladys took off for the back door, which meant Reed had arrived.

A few minutes later she glimpsed the top of his head coming through the gate.

She opened the door and Gladys dashed out, tail in full swing, to greet him and lead him to the house.

He took one look at Paige and raised his brows. "Wow, you look gorgeous."

She felt the heat rise in her cheeks. "Thank you. Shall we walk to the restaurant? It's a pretty mild evening."

He nodded, "Sure, that sounds good."

He helped her with her coat and gave Gladys a pat on the head before taking Paige's arm in his. He made sure the gate was secured, and they rounded the side of the house, where they had an unobstructed view of the square.

"It really is breathtakingly beautiful," he said, gesturing toward the tree.

"I know. I was just thinking the same thing when I looked out the window earlier. I finally see what Mom always knew."

They walked down to the end of Main Street and ducked into the bistro.

Candles glowed atop each of the tables, covered in crisp white tablecloths, and the same deep teal color of the entry doors was duplicated in the raised-panel wood walls that ran along the sides of the restaurant. The effect was cozy and quite charming.

A hostess led them to their table, next to the window that looked out on Main Street and framed a beautiful tree, its trunk and branches wrapped with tiny white lights.

Reed helped Paige off with her coat and slid out her chair for her. The hostess handed them menus and promised their server would be with them soon.

Moments later, a young man filled their water glasses and delivered a basket of warm bread and a dish of chilled butter.

"My name is Roland and I'll do my best to make your dinner memorable tonight," he said before making a quiet retreat to leave them alone.

At first Paige had thought he might be French, but when he spoke, it was clear he wasn't. He had the same Vermont accent that she did, even though his manner of speaking was much more eloquent and lyrical than hers.

When he was gone, Reed eyed the menu. "This looks promising. I can't believe Linden Falls is home to a place like this. You'd almost think you were in Paris."

"Have you been?"

"Yes, a few times. I take it you haven't?"

She shook her head as she read the menu. "No, it's been on my bucket list, but not yet."

135

"We might have to remedy that." He winked and offered her first choice from the bread basket.

Their waiter arrived and went over a couple of specials and then took their orders. Neither opted for wine, sticking with water. They both started with the onion soup, topped with a thick layer of melted cheese, that smelled delicious.

Paige had burned the roof of her mouth on French onion soup before, so she was waiting until it cooled a bit.

"How was the city? Did your meetings go well?"

He was poking at the cheese atop his bowl. "Outside of the long drive and the insane traffic, it was a huge success." He grinned and took his first spoonful. "Ah, this is delicious."

"Did you stop and see your mom today?"

He nodded. "Yes, I stopped in when I got back to town. She said you came out on Monday night and had a nice visit. I think she's come around to the idea of selling the house. She showed me the sketch she did of the layout in the apartment." He smiled across the table. "Thank you for suggesting that. I think it helped."

"I thought it might. I believe she'll adjust to it, and if she can teach some art classes, I bet she'll flourish there."

He nodded. "It may surprise her, and she might even be happier there with all the social interaction. Now, I just need to tackle the house." He sighed and placed his empty bowl on the edge of the table.

"Jed and I can help, I'm sure. Somebody once told

me it's easier to face hard things with a friend by your side."

The busboy returned with more water and collected their empty dishes.

Reed dipped his head at Paige and chuckled. "Touché. Seriously, I will probably take you up on that. I was going to ask Jed about paying his crew to help when the time comes. I'll need a truck to haul stuff away."

"I know I can speak for him when I say consider it done. You're practically family."

He reached across the white tablecloth and gripped both of her hands in his. "Paige," he said, but was interrupted when Roland, their deceptively French-looking waiter, arrived with their entrees.

They moved their hands, and he placed the chicken with garlic mashed potatoes in front of Paige and set the platter of steak frites before Reed.

Paige inhaled the lemon and garlic white wine sauce drizzled over the chicken. "Oh, this smells so yummy."

They dug into the meal, both of them moaning with delight as they took their first bites. "I think we might have to make this one of our weekly stops," said Reed, spearing one of the sea-salted fries.

She pointed her fork at the roasted Brussels sprouts on her plate. "You should try one of these. I hate Brussels sprouts, but these are actually tasty."

He frowned, stabbed one with his fork, and took a

bite. "You're right, they're not bad. It's the bacon. It makes anything edible."

Almost an hour passed as they ate and chatted, with Paige telling him about the holiday cards she was making. "I've decided to reach out to my old contacts and try to get a few illustrating jobs lined up for winter. After Christmas, the store will be slow and I'll need something to keep busy, plus the income would be nice."

"That's wonderful news and makes sense. You're so talented, and between you and me, you were Mom's favorite student." He winked at her. "I'm glad you decided to get back to your art. If it's anything like writing, it can be quite therapeutic."

She smiled and nodded. "Yes, I'm looking forward to escaping into my own little world of happiness."

The busboy cleared the table and the waiter dropped off a dessert menu. Paige scanned the selections, her eyes going wide. "Oh, wow, they make it hard to resist."

"Uh, Paige, before dessert, I need to ask you something." He reached across the table again and took her hand. "Part of the reason I went back to the city was to tell my editor I wasn't going to return to New York. I'm going to stay here in Linden Falls."

Her eyes sparkled in the glow of the candlelight. "That's wonderful news."

"Everything, everyone I care about is here. There's nothing for me in the city. I can work from anywhere, and although I enjoy meeting with my editor and the marketing team in person, with technology we can video chat whenever we need to. If I have to make the trip in once a year or whatever, I can do that."

"It sounds like you've given it a lot of thought," Paige said. She tried to control her suddenly out-of-control pulse and the pounding of her heart.

He took a deep breath. "I have. All this with my mom, with your mom, has made me realize I need to do more than spend all my time holed up in my apartment writing nonstop and tackling the next deadline as soon as I finish the current one. I don't have much of a life and I intend to change that, starting now."

The waiter approached the table and Reed waved him away. "Paige, I have something else to say."

She nodded, too nervous to speak.

"Over these last weeks, I've fallen in love with you. I should say, again. I think I always loved you but was too young and clueless to realize it. It's more than about my mother and the charm I forgot this town has. I want to stay in Linden Falls because of you. I'd like nothing more than a chance to build a life together. Will you do me the honor of marrying me?"

Her mouth gaped open as he reached into his pocket and pulled out a small velvet box, the iconic color of blue telegraphing the famous store it came from.

He popped open the lid, and the brilliant diamond glittered in the glow of the candle, but not more than the tears that she strained to keep from falling.

She clutched her hand to her chest. "Oh, Reed, it's gorgeous. I'm just so shocked."

"Happy shocked, I hope?" His brow furrowed.

She nodded, tears finally clouding her eyes and springing forward. "Very happy. I've had the same feelings about you. I couldn't figure out if it was just the nostalgia and all that has happened or if it was more. I was dreading the day you had to leave, so this just makes me so happy." Tears plopped onto her cheeks.

He wiggled the ring box in front of her. "So, is that a yes?" He gritted his teeth and gave her a questioning look.

She wouldn't make him wait a second longer.

"Yes, yes," she said, her answer full of happy laughter.

He leaned across the table and kissed her, then rested his forehead against hers. "You had me worried there for a minute."

He took the ring from the box and slipped it onto her finger.

Paige's breath caught as she held her hand out and the large cushion-cut diamond caught the light. "It's stunning, Reed."

He smiled, his face now relaxed and serene. "I know it seems fast, but it's been, what, over thirty years in the making? I just couldn't leave and make the same mistake again. You make me happy, Paige, and I promise I'll do everything in my power to make you happy, until my last breath."

Roland returned with two flutes of champagne and

a huge slice of trois chocolate cake with two dessert forks. "Compliments of the house and congratulations on your engagement. And if you'd both approve, I'd love to mark this moment with some special words."

Reed nodded for him to go ahead.

"*Aimer, c'est vivre; aimer, c'est voir; aimer, c'est être.* Love, it is life; love, it is sight; love, is to be," Roland said with a flourish of his arm. "And those are words written by Victor Hugo."

They thanked him and each slipped a fork into the decadent three-layer chocolate mousse cake.

"Poetry and chocolate," Paige said. "What could be better?"

As she tasted the first bite, she sat up straighter in her chair. "Oh, wait. Does this mean I can finally know your secret? If I'm going to be your wife, I'm sure the publishing company will understand, won't they?"

He chuckled and reached behind him to the inside pocket of his coat. He pulled out a package, wrapped in plain brown paper and tied with an orange ribbon. "For you, my love."

She put down her fork and ripped it open. She gasped when she saw the cover and looked at the author's name, Amelia Summerfield.

"Oh, my gosh." She looked up at his smiling eyes and he brought his finger to his lips. She whispered, "You write women's fiction? I've read almost all of these but didn't think of them. I was thinking more of thrillers."

She opened the book and inside was a card tied to a

glittery orange ribbon. She held up the ribbon and read the card. *Please help my sweet daughter find happiness and the strength to wish again.*

She bit into her lip, recognizing her mother's handwriting, and looked up at Reed, tears falling onto her cheeks. He brushed his fingers against her arm. "The first day I came to town, I walked under the tree and it fell onto my jacket."

"It's my mom's wish." She shook her head in wonder as she stared at the paper, running her finger over the writing.

"I realized that when I came to the bookstore and saw all her handwritten signs. I like to think this was all her doing."

She leaned across the table and kissed him again. "I think you are right—it was them. Mom and her Wishing Tree."

EPILOGUE

*T*he sound of the bell tinkling above the door of the bookstore made Paige look up from brewing her cup of tea. The young woman standing in the doorway waved her hand and smiled. "I wasn't sure if you were open yet. I just wanted to take a look at your DIY home remodeling section." She stepped inside and Gladys hurried to greet her.

"Come on in. I'm just brewing a cup of tea. Would you like one?"

She glanced at her watch. "Sure, I have time for one before I head to work." She looked around. "Wow. This place hasn't changed much. I spent lots of time in here growing up. My mom, too. Irene Olson. I'm Pam."

"Nice to see you, Pam. I'm Paige and I remember your mom. She was so kind to me at my mom's funeral. Irene's such a talented seamstress, and my mom has several of her table runners in her linen cupboard."

Pam's smile faded. "She told me about Margot's passing. I'm so sorry to hear that. She was a special lady and a big loss to the town. It feels surreal not to see her standing somewhere in here, filing books or building displays. Or chatting up the customers. Even the children at the elementary school loved to come to her read-aloud sessions. I'm pretty sure she converted a lot of kids over from video games to reading. She truly was one of the most hospitable people I ever met."

Paige sighed and came from around the counter to hand Pam a mug. "I know. It feels empty in here without her cheerful energy. It's been quite the shock, but each day it gets a bit easier. The shop"—she glanced down at Gladys, who was leaning against her thigh—"and this sweet girl give me a purpose and something to focus on instead of being sad."

Pam smiled. "Coming home to Linden Falls wasn't something I imagined happening either, but here I am."

Paige chuckled. "We have that in common."

Pam looked down at Paige's hand. "I thought we had something else in common, too. Your engagement ring is gorgeous. It's hard to be single in a small town. Everyone is always trying to match you up with someone, no matter how much you tell them you aren't interested."

Paige blushed. "I wasn't exactly looking...Reed is an old friend and we reconnected. Recently, actually."

"Lucky you. I probably sounded like I was wishing you were single. It's just that I haven't been so lucky, and my divorce sometimes leaves me coming across as jaded about love."

"Well, are you?" Paige asked.

"Am I what? Jaded about love?" she stammered, looking away for a second before coming back to Paige. "I don't know. I'm not so sure I believe in it anymore. Not after...well, let's just say that it's been... well, it's been a hard year." She suddenly looked horrified. "Wow. I'm so sorry, Paige. Here I am talking about how horrible my divorce was and you've recently lost your mother. I'm an idiot."

Paige put a hand out and touched Pam's arm. "No, don't feel that way. I completely understand the whole relationship thing. It can be so hard. After losing my husband, I never thought I'd find the real thing again either. I still feel like pinching myself sometimes to see if this is really my life. I think I was exactly in your shoes not too long ago. At my age, I never dreamed I'd find someone who wanted the same things I do or wanted to do them with me. Or that I could trust."

Pam cleared her throat. "No, really, I'm fine. My life is full enough with my work at the gym and all the projects I've got going on at home. I actually don't have time for anything else." She laughed awkwardly, then pointed out the window. "I see our famous Wishing Tree is still the main attraction. I can't understand how everyone still believes in the magic of it. It's just silly."

Paige followed her gaze. "Trust me, I used to feel the same way. I had lost hope in that tree long ago, but now…" Paige gestured to two chairs where Gladys had moved and lay stretched in front of them. "I'm a believer. If you've got time, I'll tell you why."

To learn more about Pam and what brings her back to Linden Falls, read WORKOUT WISHES AND VALENTINE KISSES, the next book in series by Barbara Hinske.

⟫⟫

Don't miss any books in the Wishing Tree series:

★ Don't miss a Wishing Tree book! ★

Book 1: The Wishing Tree – prologue book
Book 2: I Wish.. by Amanda Prowse
Book 3: Wish You Were Here by Kay Bratt
Book 4: Wish Again by Tammy L. Grace
Book 5: Workout Wishes & Valentine Kisses by Barbara Hinske
Book 6: A Parade of Wishes by Camille Di Maio
Book 7: Careful What You Wish by Ashley Farley
Book 8: Gone Wishing by Jessie Newton
Book 9: Wishful Thinking by Kay Bratt
Book 10: Overdue Wishes by Tammy L. Grace
Book 11: A Whole Heap of Wishes by Amanda Prowse
Book 12: Wishes of Home by Barbara Hinske
Book 13: Wishful Witness by Tonya Kappes

WE ALSO INVITE you to join us in our My Book Friends group on Facebook. It's a great place to chat about all things bookish and learn more about our founding authors.

FROM THE AUTHOR

Thank you for reading the fourth book in THE WISHING TREE SERIES. It's been a fun project, working with my author friends from My Book Friends, and I hope you'll read all the books in the series. They are all wonderful stories centered around a special tree in Linden Falls. If you enjoyed this story, I hope you'll explore more of my work. You can find all my books on Amazon and many of them on other major retailers. The Winey Widows from WISH AGAIN also feature in my GLASS BEACH COTTAGE SERIES, when they take a trip to the coast of Washington and spend some time at the cottage.

If you're a fan of mysteries, I write the COOPER HARRINGTON DETECTIVE NOVELS, a private detective series of whodunit murder mysteries. If you enjoy women's fiction, you'll want to try my best-selling HOMETOWN HARBOR SERIES, filled with stories of friendship and family, set in the islands of the Pacific Northwest.

The two books I've written as Casey Wilson, A DOG'S HOPE and A DOG'S CHANCE, both have received enthusiastic support from my readers and, if you're a dog lover, are must-reads.

If you enjoy holiday stories, be sure to check out my CHRISTMAS IN SILVER FALLS SERIES and HOME-TOWN CHRISTMAS SERIES. They are small-town Christmas stories of hope, friendship, and family. I'm also one of the authors of the best-selling SOUL SISTERS AT CEDAR MOUNTAIN LODGE SERIES, centered around a woman who opens her heart and home to four foster girls one Christmas.

I'm a huge dog lover and include dogs in all my books. I'd love to send you my exclusive interview with the canine companions in my Hometown Harbor Series as a thank-you for joining my exclusive group of readers. You can sign up for my newsletter at this link: https://wp.me/P9umIy-e

I hope you'll connect with me on social media. You can find me on Facebook, where I have a page and a special group for my readers, and follow me on Amazon and BookBub so you'll know when I have a new release or a deal. Be sure to download the free novella HOMETOWN HARBOR: THE BEGINNING. It's a prequel to FINDING HOME that I know you'll enjoy.

If you did enjoy this book or any of my other books,

I'd be grateful if you took a few minutes to leave a short review on Amazon, BookBub, or Goodreads.

ABOUT THE AUTHOR

Tammy L. Grace is the *USA Today* best-selling and award-winning author of the Cooper Harrington Detective Novels, the best-selling Hometown Harbor Series, and the Glass Beach Cottage Series, along with several sweet Christmas novellas. Tammy also writes under the pen name of Casey Wilson for Bookouture and Grand Central Publishing. You'll find Tammy online at www.tammylgrace.com where you can join her mailing list and be part of her exclusive group of readers. She invites you to join her in My Book Friends, a fun Facebook group where readers and authors chat about all things bookish. Connect with Tammy on social media at the links below.

facebook.com/tammylgrace.books

instagram.com/authortammylgrace

amazon.com/author/tammylgrace

bookbub.com/authors/tammy-l-grace

Made in United States
North Haven, CT
07 November 2023

43736500R00104